ROBIN SLOAN is the author of *Mr. Penumbra's 24-Hour Bookstore.* He grew up in Michigan and now splits his time between the Bay Area and the internet.

ALSO BY ROBIN SLOAN

Mr. Penumbra's 24-Hour Bookstore

Ajax Penumbra 1969

Additional Praise for
SOURDOUGH

"As he did in *Mr. Penumbra's 24-Hour Bookstore*, Robin Sloan will have readers looking for magic in the mundane."
—Nora Horvath, *Real Simple*

"Baking, foodie culture, and a club made up of women named Lois all figure into this charming story about a coder slogging away at a trendy tech company. When friends give her some sourdough starter and she begins making her own bread, everything changes." —*Entertainment Weekly*

"Fascinating . . . Insightful . . . One of the more cogent novels this year on the fertile tensions that exist between culture and technology." —Andy Newman, *The Atlantic*

"If you've ever been confused about what's artificial and what's authentic—can you really tell anymore?—*Sourdough* is a book for you." —Jeffery Gleaves, *The Paris Review Daily*

"The same vibrancy that pervades Sloan's first book, *Mr. Penumbra's 24-Hour Bookstore*, finds its way in *Sourdough*. . . . It's a novel stuffed full of ideas, but it never gets bogged down by them, thanks to the pleasant clip and voice that Sloan employs throughout." —Kevin Nguyen, *GQ*

"Sloan's prose is sharp, and his critiques of capitalism, Silicon Valley, and foodie culture are finely cut." —Everdeen Mason, *The Washington Post*

"On the crust, *Sourdough* is a buddy book . . . but slice a little deeper, and you will discover, *Sourdough* is a novel about work. . . . Sloan's sense of place is palpable, and his prose is dusted with luxurious lines to be savored."

—David LaBounty, *The Dallas Morning News*

"Delightful . . . Equal measures techie and foodie fodder, a perfect parable for our times." —*San Francisco Magazine*

"[*Sourdough*] fuses the story of worker alienation and embodied consciousness and microbiomes and microbiology with robotics in a beautiful way. . . . A Robert Pirsig or Armistead Maupin kind of novel, but it's about robotic arms and sourdough bread!" —Cory Doctorow, *Boing Boing*

"A flour-dusted hero's journey into the Bay Area's epicurean underworld, and a playful, odd tale about food as a sustainer of life in its many forms . . . A familiar world embellished by a particularly inventive mind."

—Chelsea Leu, *San Francisco Chronicle*

"Filled with crisp humor and weird but endearing characters . . . Perfect for those who like a little magic with their meals."

—*Booklist* (starred review)

"A wild, geeky, flour-dusted ride through the oddball food and techie communities of San Francisco . . . A winning story that—like its namesake bread—carries a satisfying tang."

—*Shelf Awareness*

"How many novels can boast an obstreperous sourdough starter as a key character? A delightful and heartfelt read."

—*Library Journal*

"Sloan's comic but smart tone never flags, and Lois is an easy hero to root for." —*Kirkus Reviews*

"Sloan has imagined a funny and curious novel unlike anything else, a perfect combination of self-discovery through all sorts of weird passions. Like truly good sourdough, this is the perfectly tangy, chewy, and airy addition to anyone's reading list—minus the gluten and calories, of course."

—*BookPage*

"Through narrative and email correspondence, Sloan captures contemporary work environments, current reality, and future trends. . . . [*Sourdough*] offers much to savor."

—*Publishers Weekly*

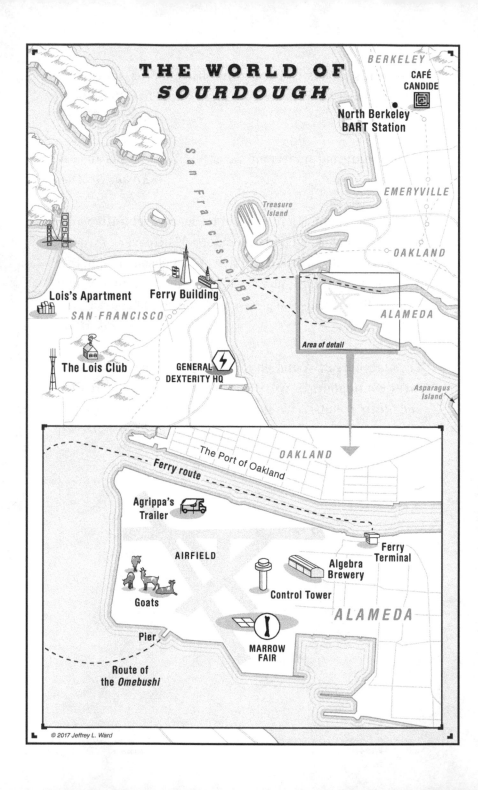

SOURDOUGH

OR, LOIS AND HER
ADVENTURES IN THE
UNDERGROUND MARKET

A NOVEL

ROBIN SLOAN

Picador

MCD

FARRAR, STRAUS AND GIROUX

NEW YORK

SOURDOUGH. Copyright © 2017 by Robin Sloan. All rights reserved. For information, address Picador, 175 Fifth Avenue, New York, N.Y. 10010. Map copyright © 2017 by Jeffrey L. Ward.

picadorusa. c om • instagram. c om / picador
twitter. c om / picadorusa • facebook. c om / picadorusa

Picador® is a U.S. registered trademark and is used by Macmillan Publishing Group, LLC, under license from Pan Books Limited.

For book club information, please visit facebook.com/ picadorbookclub or email marketing@picadorusa.com.

Designed by Abby Kagan

The Library of Congress has cataloged the MCD edition as follows:

Names: Sloan, Robin, 1979– author.
Title: Sourdough / Robin Sloan.
Description: First edition. | New York: MCD/Farrar, Straus and Giroux, 2017.
Identifiers: LCCN 2016059400 | ISBN 9780374203108 (hardcover) | ISBN 9780374716431 (ebook)
Classification: LCC PS3619.L6278 S67 2017 | DDC 813'.6– dc23
LC record available at https://lccn.loc.gov/2016059400

Picador Paperback ISBN 978-1-250-19275-2

Our books may be purchased in bulk for promotional, educational, or business use. Please contact your local bookseller or the Macmillan Corporate and Premium Sales Department at 1-800-221-7945, extension 5442, or by email at MacmillanSpecialMarkets@macmillan.com.

First published by MCD, an imprint of Farrar, Straus and Giroux

First Picador Edition: September 2018

For Kathryn

ACKNOWLEDGMENTS

Thanks to Dan Bouk, Patrick Ewing, Andrew Fitzgerald, Wilson Miner, Kiyash Monsef, Jim Ray, Sarah Rich, Brad Thomason, and Kathryn Tomajan: first readers.

Thanks also to Norma Barksdale, Maya Binyam, Rebecca Caine, Rodrigo Corral, Rebecca Gardner, Brian Gittis, Debra Helfand, Naomi Huffman, Abby Kagan, Roberta Klugman, Spenser Lee, Will Roberts, Jeff Seroy, Lisa Silverman, and Rob Sternitzky: collaborators.

Thanks, most of all, to Sarah Burnes and Sean McDonald: instigators.

SOURDOUGH

NUMBER ONE EATER

IT WOULD HAVE BEEN nutritive gel for dinner, same as always, if I had not discovered stuck to my apartment's front door a paper menu advertising the newly expanded delivery service of a neighborhood restaurant.

I was just home from work and my face felt brittle from stress—this wasn't unusual—and I would not normally have been interested in anything unfamiliar. My nightly ration of Slurry waited within.

But the menu intrigued me. The words were written in a dark, confident script—actually, two scripts: each dish was described once using the alphabet I recognized and again using one I didn't, vaguely Cyrillic-seeming with a profusion of dots and curling connectors. In either case, the menu was compact: available was the *Spicy Soup* or a *Spicy Sandwich* or a *Combo (double spicy)*, all of which, the menu explained, were vegetarian.

At the top, the restaurant's name was written in humongous, exuberant letters: *CLEMENT STREET SOUP AND SOURDOUGH*. At the bottom, there was a phone number and the promise of quick delivery. Clement Street was just a few blocks away. The menu charmed me, and as a result, my night, and my life, bent off on a different track.

I dialed the number and my call was answered immediately. It was a man's voice, slightly breathless. "Clement Street Soup and Sourdough! Okay to hold?"

I said yes, and music played—a song in some other language. Clement Street was a polyglot artery that pulsed with Cantonese, Burmese, Russian, Thai, and even scraps of Gaelic. This was none of those.

The voice returned. "Okay! Hello! What can I make for you?"

I ordered the double spicy.

I CAME TO SAN FRANCISCO from Michigan, where I was raised and educated and where my body's functioning was placid and predictable, mostly.

My father was a database programmer for General Motors who liked his work and had endeavored to surround me with computers from toddlerhood onward, and whose plan succeeded because I never thought of anything except following his path, especially at a time when programming was taking on a sheen of dynamism and computer science departments were wooing young women aggressively. It's nice to be wooed.

It helped that I was good at it. I liked the rhythm of challenge and solution; it felt very satisfying to solve programming problems. For two summers during college, I interned at Crowley Control Systems, a company in Southfield that provided motor control software for one of Chevrolet's electric cars, and when I graduated, there was a job waiting for me.

The work was minutely specified and cautiously tested, and it had the feeling of laying bricks: put them down carefully, because you won't get another chance. The computer on my desk was old, used by at least two programmers before me, but the codebase was modern and interesting. I kept a picture of my parents next to my monitor, along with a tiny cactus I'd named Kubrick. I bought a house two towns over, in Ferndale.

Then I was recruited. A woman contacted me through my stubby LinkedIn profile—her own identifying her as a talent associate at a company called General Dexterity in San Francisco—with a request for an exploratory phone call, which I accepted. I could hear her bright smile through the speaker. General Dexterity, she said, designed industry-leading robot arms for laboratories and factories. The company needed programmers with a background in motor control, and in San Francisco, she said, such programmers were rare. She explained that a software sieve had flagged my résumé as promising and that she agreed with the computer's assessment.

Here's a thing I believe about people my age: we are the children of Hogwarts, and more than anything, we just want to be sorted.

Sitting there in my car in the little parking lot behind Crowley Control Systems on West 10 Mile Road in Southfield, my world cracked open a tiny bit. It was only a hairline fracture, but that was enough to see through.

On the other end of the line, the talent associate conjured difficult problems suited to only the fiercest intellects. She conjured generous benefits and free food and, oh, was I vegetarian? Not anymore, no. But maybe I could try again, in California. She conjured sunshine. The sky above the Crowley parking lot was gray and drippy like the undercarriage of a car.

And—no conjuring here—the talent associate made an offer. It was a salary that represented more money than both of my parents currently earned, combined. I was a year out of college. I was being wooed again.

Ten months into a Michigan-sized mortgage, I sold my house in Ferndale at a very small loss. I hadn't hung a single thing on the walls. When I said goodbye to my parents, I cried. College had been less than an hour away, so this was the real departure. I set out across the country with all my belongings in the back of my car and my desk cactus strapped into the passenger scat.

I drove west through the narrow pass in the Rockies, crossed the dusty nothing of Nevada, and crashed into the verdant, vertical shock of California. I was agog. Southeastern Michigan is flat, almost concave; here was a world with a z-axis.

In San Francisco, a temporary apartment waited for me, and so did the talent associate, who met me on the sidewalk in front of General Dexterity's brick-faced headquarters. She was tiny, barely five feet tall, but when she took my hand, her grip was viselike. "Lois Clary! Welcome! You're going to love it here!"

The first week was amazing. Grouped with a dozen other newly Dextrous (as we were encouraged to call ourselves), I filled out health insurance forms and accepted a passel of phantasmal stock options and sat through recitations of the company's short history. I saw the founder's original prototype robot arm, a beefy three-jointed limb almost as tall as me, set up in a little shrine in the center of the cafeteria. You could call out "Arm, change task. Say hello!" and it would wave a wide, eager greeting.

I learned the anatomy of the software I'd be working on, called ArmOS. I met my manager, Peter, who shook my hand with a grip even firmer than the talent associate's. An in-house apartment broker found me a place on Cabrillo Street in San Francisco's Richmond District for which I would pay rent fully four times larger than my mortgage in Michigan. The broker dropped the keys into my hand and said, "It's not a lot of space, but you won't be spending much time there!"

General Dexterity's founder, an astonishingly young man named Andrei, walked our group across Townsend Street to the Task Acquisition Center, a low-slung building that had once been a parking garage. The cement floor was still mottled with oil spots. Now, instead of cars in long lines, there were robot arms parked thirty to a row. Their plastic cladding was colored Dextrous blue, the contours friendly and capable with just the faintest suggestion of biceps—gentle swells marked with General Dexterity's logo, an affable lightning bolt.

The arms were all going at once, sweeping and grasping and nudging and lifting. If it was supposed to impress us: it worked.

All of these were repetitive gestures, Andrei explained, currently executed by human muscles and human minds. Repetition was the enemy of creativity, he said. Repetition belonged to robots.

We were on a quest to end work.

And it would involve: a shit ton of work.

My orientation week ended on Friday night with celebratory beers and a ping-pong tournament against one of the robot arms, which of course emerged victorious. Then my job began. Not the following Monday. The next morning. Saturday.

I had the feeling of being sucked—*floop*—into a pneumatic tube.

The programmers at General Dexterity were utterly unlike my colleagues at Crowley, who had been middle-aged and chilled-out, and who enjoyed nothing as much as a patient explanation. The Dextrous were in no way patient. Many of them were college dropouts; they had been in a hurry to get here, and they were in a hurry now to be done, and rich. They were almost entirely young men, bony and cold-eyed, wraiths in Japanese denim and limited-edition sneakers. They started late in the morning, then worked past midnight. They slept at the office.

I hated the idea of it, but some nights I, too, succumbed to the cushy couches upholstered in Dextrous blue. Some nights, I'd lie there, staring up at the ceiling—the exposed ductwork, the rainbow braids of fiber channel ferrying data around the office—and feel a knot in my stomach that wouldn't loosen. I would think I had to poop and I would go squat on a toilet, doing nothing. The motion sensor would time out and the lights would click off, leaving me in darkness. Sometimes I would sit like that for a while. Then a line of code would occur to me, and I would limp back to my desk to tap it out.

At Crowley Control Systems in Southfield, the message we received from Clark Crowley, delivered in an amble around the office every month or so, was: Keep up the fine work, folks! At General Dexterity in San Francisco, the message we received from Andrei, delivered in a quantitative business update every Tuesday and Thursday, was: We are on a mission to remake the conditions of human labor, so push harder, all of you.

I began to wonder if, in fact, I knew how to push hard. In Michigan, my colleagues all had families and extremely serious hobbies. Here, the wraiths were stripped bare: human-shaped generators of CAD and code. I tried to emulate them, but something hitched inside me. I couldn't get my turbine spinning.

In the months that followed, I had the sense of some vital resource dwindling, and I tried to ignore it. My colleagues had been toiling at this pace for three years without a pause, and I was already flagging after a single San Francisco summer? I was supposed to be one of the bright new additions, the fresh-faced ones.

My face was not fresh.

My hair had gone flat and thin.

My stomach hurt.

In my apartment on Cabrillo Street, I existed mostly in a state of catatonic recovery, brain flaccid, cells gasping. My parents were far away, locked in the frame of a video chat window. I didn't have any friends in San Francisco aside from a handful of Dextrous, but they were just as traumatized as I was. My apartment was small and dark, and I paid too much for it, and the internet was slow.

TWELVE MINUTES after I had called it in, my order from Clement Street Soup and Sourdough arrived, carried to my door by a young man with a sweet face half hidden inside a ketchup-colored motorcycle helmet. A soft *oonce-oonce* of

9

music emanated from within the helmet, and he bobbed to the beat.

He boomed his greeting in a heavy, hard-to-place accent: "Good evening, my friend!"

Greatest among us are those who can deploy "my friend" to total strangers in a way that is not hollow, but somehow real and deeply felt; those who can make you, within seconds of first contact, believe it.

I dug in my pocket for cash, and then, as I paid him, I thought to ask, "What kind of food is this?"

His face lit up like a neon sign. "It is the food of the Mazg! I hope you like it. If not, call again. My brother will make it better next time." He jogged toward his motorcycle but, halfway there, turned back to say, "You will like it, though." Above the rev of the engine he waved and repeated: "You will like it!"

Inside my apartment, on my kitchen countertop—utterly bare, free from any sign of food preparation or, really, human habitation—I unwrapped the sandwich and opened the soup and consumed the first combo (double spicy) of my life.

If Vietnamese pho's healing powers, physical and psychic, make traditional chicken noodle soup seem like dishwater—and they do—then this spicy soup, in turn, dishwatered pho. It was an elixir. The sandwich was spicier still, thin-sliced vegetables slathered with a fluorescent red sauce, the burn buffered by thick slabs of bread artfully toasted.

First my stomach unclenched, and then my brain. I let loose a long sigh that transformed into a rippling burp, which made me laugh out loud, alone, in my kitchen.

I lifted the lone magnet on my refrigerator, allowed a sheet of shiny pizza coupons to fall to the floor, and stuck the new menu reverently in its place.

I CALLED CLEMENT STREET SOUP AND SOURDOUGH again the next night, and the next. Then I skipped a night, feeling self-conscious, but I ordered again the night after that. For all its spiciness, the food sat perfectly in my traumatized stomach.

In the month that followed, I learned about it bit by bit:

- The restaurant was operated by two brothers.
- Beoreg, with the sweet voice and the perfect English, answered the phone and cooked the food.
- Chaiman, with the sweet face and the earbuds never not leaking dance music, rode the motorcycle and delivered the food.
- When pressed for more information on "the food of the Mazg," Chaiman would only laugh and say, "It's famous!"
- Beoreg and Chaiman had been slinging spicy soups and/or sandwiches in San Francisco for just over a year.
- They possessed no storefront: they cooked where they lived, in an apartment whose precise location they were reluctant to disclose.
- Chaiman said, "It is okay. Just not legal. Definitely okay, though."
- With the double spicy, one bonus slab of sourdough bread was included, always, for dunking in your soup.
- That bread was the secret of the whole operation. Beoreg baked it himself every day.
- That bread was life.

Most nights, I called ahead and waited on hold (though I was recognized, and the greeting from brother Beoreg was not "Okay to hold?" but "Lois! Hi! I have to put you on hold. Just a second, I promise") with the music in another language I'd grown to appreciate—it was sad, in a nice way—and then, rescued from purgatory, I placed my order (the same order every time), and when brother Chaiman brought it on his motorcycle, I greeted him warmly and tipped him generously, then carried my double spicy inside to eat it standing, my eyes watering from the heat and the happiness.

One Friday, after a particularly shattering day at the office, in which my code reviews had all come back red with snotty comments, and my manager, Peter, had gently inquired about the pace of my refactoring ("perhaps not sufficiently turbo-charged"), I arrived home in a swirl of angst, with petulance and self-recrimination locked in ritual combat to determine which would ruin my night. On the phone with Beoreg, I ordered my food with a rattling sigh, and when his brother arrived at my door, he carried something different: a more compact tub containing a fiery red broth and not one but two slabs of bread for dipping. "Secret spicy," he whispered. The soup was so hot it burned the frustration out of me, and I went to bed feeling like a fresh plate, scalded and scraped clean.

Is it an exaggeration to say Clement Street Soup and Sourdough saved me? At night, instead of fitfully reviewing the day's errors while my stomach swam and churned, I . . . fell asleep. My course steadied. I had taken on ballast in the form of spicy broth and fragrant bread and, maybe, two new friends, or sort-of-friends, or something.

12

Then they went away.

It was on a Wednesday in September that I dialed the number and was greeted by Beoreg, who said "Okay to hold?" as if he didn't recognize me, then abandoned me to the sad-but-nice music for a very long time, so long in fact I suspected he'd forgotten me. When he came back on the line, he accepted my order dutifully and told me his brother would bring it soon. "Goodbye," he murmured before hanging up. He'd never actually said that before.

When Chaiman knocked on my door, his sweet face was morose. He wasn't listening to any music. The night seemed suddenly oppressively quiet.

"Hello, my friend," he said limply. The bag containing my double spicy dangled limply from his fingers.

I took the bag and cradled it, felt the warmth of the soup across my chest. "What's wrong?"

"We are leaving," he said. "Visas, you know?"

This was unacceptable.

"We cannot stay. I would try, but Beoreg says . . . he does not want to be hidden forever. He wants to have a real restaurant. With tables." Chaiman rolled his eyes, as if wishing to serve customers in a physical establishment constituted Versailles-level extravagance.

"We will miss you," he said. "Me and Beoreg both."

The bag in my arms crinkled, and so did the skin around my eyes. I wanted to wail, *Don't leave me! What will I eat? Who will I call?* But all I could muster was "I'm so sorry to hear about this."

He nodded. I did, too. It was September, and the air was very cold. He said, "I should tell you . . . Beoreg and I have a joke. When he gives me the bag"—he poked at the food in my arms—"and says, for Lois on Cabrillo Street, we always say together: the number one eater!"

I didn't know what that meant, but I knew I had never been one before.

"It's supposed to be nice. Because we like you. You know?"

I did.

Astride his motorcycle, Chaiman raised a hand and shook his index finger emphatically. Above the rev of the engine, he cried again: "Number one eater!"

THE SLURRY TABLE

WORK LOOKED LIKE THIS: me, sitting for twelve hours at my desk in the basement of a converted macaroni factory near the park where the Giants play. My company-issued laptop was hulking and loud, the roaring fan necessary to cool the superfast GPU within. At my desk, I hooked it into a pair of monitors, a keyboard, a tablet with stylus. No mouse. I'd learned the tablet trick from one of the patient programmers at Crowley, who recommended it as a ward against repetitive stress injury. Here at General Dexterity, the wraiths regarded it strangely. They could not yet imagine their bodies betraying them.

ArmOS was comprised of two lobes.

First there was Control, the code that told the arms how to move. It read their super-precise sensors, flexed their motor-muscles. The code was very compact and highly optimized, because any improvement to Control—a faster sensor reading, a firmer grip—applied to everything the arms did.

Then there was Task, the code that told the arms *why* to move. Task was a thrilling jumble of heuristics and hacks.

If Control was all about one thing—moving in space—then Task was about a thousand things. The module called Stacking gave the arms a theory of gravity, balance, and layers, and right next door there was the module called Glassware, a hard-coded cheat sheet containing the dimensions, to the micrometer, of the world's ten thousand most common scientific flasks and vials.

(In addition to Task and Control there was also Interface, the code that allowed users to control their arms and apply continuous ArmOS upgrades, all with a simple web app, but the other teams pitied Interface, because its work was so easy.)

My manager, Peter, had recently been promoted to oversee all of Control. I worked on the submodule responsible for Proprioception, which is, I think, a beautiful word—*pro-pri-o-cep-tion!*—and also the process by which organisms judge the position of their own body parts in space. It's a crucial sense; definitely more important than a few of the Big Five. When you walk, you look forward, not down at your feet, because you are confident they are where you expect them to be, obeying your commands. That's a pretty cool feature.

It was an unanticipated consequence of working on robot proprioception that I would often sit at my desk snaking my arms around in the air, trying to pay very close attention to what was happening. I'd close my eyes, extend a hand, lift it slowly while rotating it at the same time. What was I feeling? The weight of my own limb, yes; but also . . . a tendril of strange information. Not touch, exactly. Something else. Proprioception!

I did this quite a bit, for reasons both technical and therapeutic, and once, I opened my eyes to find Peter standing there, silently watching me propriocept. I yelped.

My persistent stomachache had been diagnosed after a consultation at General Dexterity's in-house clinic (next to the dentist and the masseuse) as stress-related. The nurse plucked a brochure from a thick stack; its title, printed in Dextrous blue, was *Taking Care of Yourself While You're Changing the World.*

It was Peter who recommended switching to the liquid meal replacement that he and many of the other programmers preferred, and that seemed easier to digest under the circumstances, which were extreme and unrelenting.

"Slurry," he said. "It's outstanding."

Slurry was a nutritive gel manufactured by an eponymous company even newer than General Dexterity. Dispensed in waxy green Tetra Paks, it had the consistency of a thick milkshake. It was nutritionally complete and rich with probiotics. It was fully dystopian.

I signed up for a trial month using a coupon code obtained from Peter and had my subscription delivered directly to the office. I was not alone. On the day I picked it up in the mail room, there was an enormous ziggurat of green Tetra Paks waiting on a shipping pallet. The gel tasted like burnt almonds and it did sit better in my stomach than the regular food in the cafeteria; it also rescued me from the endless teeter-totter between salad bar and paella station.

There was another benefit, which was social. At mealtimes, I sat in the Slurry corner of the cafeteria, where a not-insignificant fraction of the Dextrous gathered to furtively slurp our gray gel. The group around my table became my first shaky scaffolding of office friendship. Peter was our chieftain, and he was in fact sponsored by Slurry, his deluxe subscription provided free as long as he continued to place in the top five in his age group at approved athletic events (10K races, triathlons, caber tosses) and do so wearing bright green Slurry-branded spandex. His subscription was a bleeding-edge formulation with occasionally noxious side effects; he consumed it three times a day, seven days a week.

The rest of us ate Slurry only two or three days a week. The other days, we slunk into the lunch line to select our preferred fried chicken parts under Chef Kate's woeful gaze.

Besides Peter, there was Garrett, a pale and intense programmer on the internationalization team; Benjamin, a security specialist who worked to ensure that the robot arms couldn't be hacked; Anton, a sales associate burdened with a deeply unfortunate Bluetooth earpiece; and Arjun, a sprightly interface designer, also from Michigan, who became the first of the Dextrous I dared to call my friend. In addition to our interactions at the Slurry table, Arjun and I sometimes migrated to a bar farther down Townsend Street after leaving the office for ten p.m. beers and cheese fries. Peter did not approve.

During a lull in the conversation around the table—they were many; we were awkward—I told my comrades in slurpage the sad news about Clement Street Soup and Sourdough.

"I don't eat bread," Peter said preemptively.

"Didn't it hurt your stomach?" asked Garrett.

It had not. "The soup was really spicy, but it was balanced somehow. And I really liked the guys who made it." My cheeks felt tight, and I knew I was emitting a pulse of emotion that was too much for this crowd, so I said, "Back to Slurry for dinner!" and took a gurgling slurp from the Tetra Pak.

I COULDN'T FACE Proprioception or ArmOS or any of it, so I walked across Townsend Street to the Task Acquisition Center.

All the arms faced different scenarios erected on workbenches wheeled and locked into place: one was an array of test tubes, as in a lab; another, a disassembled phone, as in a factory; another, an open cardboard box, as in a warehouse; and on and on. Arms had vacuums, arms had drills, arms had nothing but their bare six-fingered hands. The training floor clicked and whirred and whined and thwacked. Above the din, the occasional human curse.

At each bench there was an instructor, moving an arm through a sequence of motions, demonstrating how a procedure unfolded: the lift and shake of a test tube; the pick and place of a phone assembly; the pack and seal of a box, which was a job for two arms together, punctuated by the *skritchhh* of tape.

The trainers were contractors, very well compensated— but only temporarily. Each lab technician or factory worker or logistics specialist would teach one robot arm how to perform one task impeccably, under many different conditions, variously adverse. When the task had been mastered, it would be integrated into ArmOS, and in that moment, every General Dexterity arm on the planet would become that much more capable.

There were trainers outside this building, too. In addition to all the built-in capabilities of ArmOS, there was a marketplace for skill extensions—things more niche than we could ever imagine. How to swirl a petri dish containing a particular strain of bacteria. How to insert a fuel rod safely into a nuclear reactor. How to sew the laces into a football. Whole companies had formed around some of these tasks. The fuel rod people had just three customers, and they were rich.

I paused for a moment to watch the arms at work, and in their subtlest motions I could see my contribution. When they swiveled in two dimensions at once, the motion was smoother than it had been a few months ago. I'd spent a lot of time poring over the PKD 2891 Stepper Motor data sheet to figure that out.

One arm, working under the supervision of a burly, bearded trainer, faced a mock kitchen countertop, bare except for a mixing bowl and a carton of eggs. *Oh no.* I pitied it.

The arm plucked an egg, brought it to the bowl, tapped it against the rim: once, gently (too gently); again, harder (still not enough); and a third time, too hard (much too hard), shell exploding against the bowl, yolk falling in orange ribbons through its fingers down both sides of the bowl, pooling on the countertop.

I was glad not to be working on Force Feedback. Even after years of work, ArmOS struggled with its gentlest touch. We would solve everything else before we solved the egg problem.

THAT DAY, I left General Dexterity earlier than I ever had before, with the sun still shining on the sidewalk outside. I activated the standard suite of office chaff: left a data sheet on my desk, opened to its third page, seemingly mid-consultation, and draped my jacket artfully across the back of my chair, indicating that I hadn't left the office—never that—but was only attending a meeting or crying in a bathroom. Normal stuff.

In fact, I hopped aboard the Muni train bound for downtown. Riding across the city, I had a knotty feeling in my chest that I briefly worried might be cardiac, but by the time the 5 bus arrived in the Richmond District, I understood it was simply sorrow.

THE CLEMENT STREET STARTER

I HAD MOURNED MY LOSS and slurped my Slurry and was buffering a dark serial drama through my slow internet connection when I heard a knock on the door, light and confident. I knew that knock.

It was Chaiman, for the first time unencumbered by his motorcycle helmet. His hair was sandy brown.

"Number one eater!" he cried.

Another figure was standing behind him, farther down the steps. This man had the same sweet face and the same sandy hair, but his skin was darker and he was thicker around the middle.

Chaiman turned to him. "Beoreg, you are too shy. Come on."

The voice on the phone! Beoreg. Chef and baker, master of the double spicy, author of my comfort. I felt like I should bow.

"We are leaving now," Chaiman said. There was a brown taxi idling in the street behind them. "But Beo had the idea to give you a gift."

"That's sweet of you," I said.

Beoreg smiled, but his gaze was fixed somewhere around

my shins. He offered an object wrapped in a scratchy kitchen towel. It was a ceramic crock, about as big as a family-size jar of peanut butter, dark green with a matching lid, the glaze shimmering iridescent.

"What is it?" It looked like the kind of vessel that might contain an ancestor's ashes, which I definitely did not want.

"It's our culture," Beoreg said softly.

Nope, I definitely did not—

"I mean 'starter,'" Beoreg corrected himself. "For making sourdough bread, you know? I brought it so you could bake your own."

I had no idea what to do with a starter.

Chaiman sensed my unease. "Beo will show you," he said. He craned his neck to peer into my apartment. "If you have a kitchen?"

I had a kitchen. I led them inside.

"It's very clean," Beoreg said. His English was flawless, with a faint clip like something from a BBC show—a new one, not a historical drama.

"I never cook," I confessed.

"Because you are the number one eater!" Chaiman hooted. He pointed gleefully at their menu, still stuck to the refrigerator.

"Do you have flour?" Beoreg asked softly.

I almost laughed. "No flour," I said. "Really. I never cook."

He nodded sharply. "No problem. I'll give you everything you need." He jogged to the door.

Chaiman had opened the refrigerator without asking and was rooting around inside. He pulled out a waxy Tetra Pak of Slurry and looked at it like it was a dead mouse.

Beoreg returned a moment later dragging an enormous wooden trunk, scarred and stickered, something from another era of travel. He unhooked its clasps and threw back the lid; inside, arrayed in a jumble, were all the accoutrements of a kitchen.

There were small long-handled cups and broad, flat pans. I saw a thick clutch of wooden spoons, their edges stained and charred, and a collection of mixing bowls nested one inside the other, padded with newspaper. There were murky glass vessels holding baby Xenomorphs (possibly they were pickles) and bright colorful boxes with labels in Arabic and Hebrew and other scripts I didn't recognize. There were tiny unmarked jars holding red and yellow powders; precursor ingredients, no doubt, to the "secret spicy." There was a cutting board upright along the back of the trunk, its surface mottled with spills and streaks and deep-notched evidence of cleaver work.

While he rummaged, Beoreg asked, "So, do you know how bread is made?"

"Sure," I said. "Basically." I knew there was flour involved. "Not really." I was an eater, not a baker.

"There's a living thing, a culture. I guess it's more American to say 'starter.' You mix the starter with the flour, along with water and salt, and it makes gas, which makes the dough rise. It gives it a certain flavor, too." Beoreg stood, holding a selection of tools. "You've had pets?"

I shook my head ruefully. The only living thing I had ever managed to support was myself, and then only barely, except for—

"Maybe a plant?"

"Yes!" I said. "I have a desk cactus."

"Okay! This culture—starter, sorry—it's like that. It's alive." He lifted the crock's lid. "See?"

The gray slime inside looked distinctly not alive. It looked like an enemy of aliveness. Like something alive things crossed the street to avoid.

"Smell," he commanded, and offered the crock, tilting it toward me. "Can you detect it?"

I took a guarded sniff, allowing no more than two or three molecules from the decrepit vessel into my nose. I equivocated. "What is it supposed to smell like?"

"Bananas, a bit. It's a very nice smell."

I sniffed again, still detected nothing, but nodded my head agreeably. "You're right. That is nice." It was the same strategy I employed at wine tastings.

Beoreg beamed. "But you have to feed it, okay? Keep it going. I'll show you how."

He plopped his selection of tools onto the countertop. First was a stout, thick-papered sack of flour, the top neatly folded and chip-clipped. "Whole flour," he said. "It has to be whole." Next came a small mixing bowl and a long-handled cup. "Measure twenty grams—just this much." He lowered the cup into the sack, leveled it with his finger. "See?" He dumped the flour into the mixing bowl, then filled the same long-handled cup with water from the tap. "The same amount." He added the water to the bowl, snatched up the last of his tools, a short wooden spoon, and started to stir.

Chaiman had been fishing around in the trunk, and he stood holding a CD jewel case. "You must play the music of the Mazg, too!" he declared.

I dug out my hulking General Dexterity laptop and felt along its edge for the CD tray I had never once used. Inside

Chaiman's jewel case there was a plain disc with its title handwritten in the mystery script of the menu. I dropped it into the tray. The laptop cleared its throat, whining and clicking, and sound began to flow from its speakers. It was the brothers' hold music, sad and inimitable, crooned in that unfamiliar language. The language of the Mazg. As it played, Beoreg and Chaiman seemed to slow down and synchronize. Chaiman's posture relaxed and Beoreg's eyes softened as he stirred.

"This is the starter's food—see?" Beoreg said, showing me how the water and flour had combined into a pale paste. "It's important to feed it every day. If you skip a day, it will be okay, but not any longer than that."

This was seeming like more and more of a commitment.

Beoreg looked me in the eye for the first time, his gaze suddenly searching. "You'll keep it alive?"

I should have backed out. I should have thanked the brothers one last time for all the combos (double spicy) and escorted them back to their taxi waiting in the street. Instead, I said: "Of course I will."

Beoreg beamed. "Good! And you can bake with it. That's great." His eyes flickered down. He handed me the mixing bowl with its pasty contents. "Here, you can feed the starter now. Your first time."

I scooped up the floury paste with the spoon, held it for a moment over the shimmering maw of the crock, then plopped it in.

"Do I stir it together?"

"Yes, until it's all mixed."

The pasty food marbled into the dark starter, and then the combined mixture faded to an even gray. I kept stirring, and stirring, until Beoreg said gently, "That's enough." He took the spoon, washed it quickly under the tap, then laid it neatly beside the mixing bowl and the long-handled cup. "All of these, you can keep."

He set the crock's lid into place with the gentleness of a parent tucking a child into bed.

I wondered what else was inside that trunk. "What about the spicy soup? Can I make that, too?"

Beoreg looked sheepish. "It's more complicated. I can write it down, maybe. Here." He scrounged for a pen, crouched in front of the refrigerator, and wrote an email address along the bottom edge of their menu. It was the same dark, sure script; that was Beoreg's handwriting. "Send me a message."

The brothers shuffled out of my apartment and into the taxi, still waving as its door clomped shut. The taxi's tires squeaked as it leapt forward into the night, carrying them to the airport or the bus station or, who knows, maybe to a boat waiting at some lonely pier.

Back in the apartment, the CD was still playing, sweet and sad.

SPARTAN STIX

L ET ME JUST ESTABLISH where I was at with the whole
cooking situation.

When I was a child, my family had no distinguishable
cuisine. I remember Happy Meal hamburgers and Hungry-
Man fried chicken. I remember the Denny's menu; we knew
that backward and forward. I remember tubs of popcorn at
the movies. Tubs of popcorn for dinner.

We possessed no stock of recipes, no traditions, no ances-
tral affinities. There was a lot of migration and drama in our
history; our line had been broken not once but many times,
like one of those gruesome accident reports, the bone shat-
tered in six places. When they put my family back together,
they left out the food.

There was one exception. My grandma Lois, for whom
I was named, did not deign to cook—she was my mother's
mother in that regard—but she did, on special occasions, bake
bread. Specifically, she baked Chicago Prison Loaf, a comi-
cally hard and dense but apparently nutritious substance that
she had learned to produce working part-time at an industrial bakery that served the Illinois Department of Correc-

tions. In my family, Chicago Prison Loaf was a joke—a grim surprise often wrapped up for Christmas in a box chosen for its resemblance to a nice sweater or a video game console. Grandma Lois did seem to genuinely enjoy eating it, toasted and slathered. The rest of us, we buttered the bread we bought at the grocery store.

My high school cafeteria offered a rotating daily menu item, but I can assure you that I never chose it. Instead: fries, fries, two orders of fries! Fries so perfectly crisp they put fast-food fries to shame, fries crusted with salt and eaten one by one, fries not merely consumed but circulated as social currency: peace offerings, seductions. Four years in that cafeteria and I ate nothing but fries. The teenage body is a miracle. How did it scrounge from those sticks of burnt starch enough vitamins and minerals to sustain me, and not just sustain me but make me grow, and grow absurdly, grow six inches, grow boobs and hips? It was a disgusting diet. I realize that now. I bow down before that body.

In college, I did not immediately realize that it was behind me. The summer before freshman year, the One Campus, One Book selection had converted me to vegetarianism, which meant the things I ate never seemed to fill me up. Armed with a dormitory meal plan, I consumed the equivalent of nine meals a day, all of them shaded brown, textured crispy. You would expect a vegetarian, perhaps, to eat vegetables; you would be disappointed. There was never on my tray a single tuft of green.

I sat in various dorm rooms with my computer science cabal, plowing through problem sets, eating whole pizzas and so-called Spartan Sticks—named for the school's mascot, and upon reflection, it may have been spelled Stix—which were just pizzas that omitted tomato sauce and compensated for its absence with more cheese and even more cheese and a flaky garlic powder that carried a hot chemical burn.

Four years of this. By the end, I was a puffy caricature of myself. As my senior year started, I did finally realize that something had gone wrong; that the teenage machine had broken down, and that my body—desperate, pushed beyond any reasonable nutritional tolerances—was simply building new parts out of salt. I tried to improve my diet, but only in the most marginal and clueless ways. I stopped ordering whole pizzas and bought family-size tubs of hummus. I consumed baby carrots by the pound.

Later, back in Southfield, I cleaned up my act somewhat. Before I was the number one eater at Clement Street Soup and Sourdough, I was a very familiar face at the Whole Foods salad bar on West 10 Mile. My creations tended to go heavy on croutons. One day, a single chicken tender found its way into the nest of lettuce. It was delicious. So closed a brief and disastrous era.

In San Francisco, I switched to Slurry, and my refrigerator looked like something out of a sci-fi movie, tight rows of shimmery Tetra Paks replenished every two weeks.

This is all to say: I'd never baked bread in my life.

THE LOIS CLUB

ICLIMBED THE HILL behind the hospital to attend a meeting of the Lois Club.

Do other names boast affiliated clubs? Certainly there is no Rachel Club. Maybe Persephones have a club. We Loises do. It's real! There are chapters scattered around the country.

My grandmother Lois LaMotte was a member of the first-ever Lois Club, in Milwaukee. Later, after she moved to Detroit to be closer to her daughter and eponymous baby granddaughter, she met another Lois waiting in line at Meijer and together they formed the Metro Detroit chapter. They advertised it in the newspaper! I attended an early meeting as an infant; there is a photo I still possess, scanned and saved, that shows a group of six white-haired women all named Lois gathered around a swaddled baby burrito who is also named Lois, their faces frozen in coos of delight. Little burrito Lois is crying.

My only conscious memory of that Lois Club comes from when I must have been nine or ten years old. I can remember the dry floral scent of someone else's grandma's house, and what then seemed to me—a shy kid—an overwhelming cacophony of laughter; unrelenting cackles. I retreated into an adjoining room, where I played my Nintendo DS. One of the Loises—I have no idea which one—stumbled upon me there, and for at least ten minutes she watched the shimmering screen silently over my shoulder.

Grandma Lois died when I was twelve, and throughout my teens my mother would gently inquire, once every couple of years, if I ever thought about attending a meeting of the Lois Club. I did not. Without Grandma Lois? Unthinkable. In any case, I'm not sure the Detroit chapter lasted long without her.

So, my first thought upon arriving in California was not: *I ought to look up the local Lois Club.* Nor was it my second thought, or my three hundred and fifty-third. It was my mother who sent me the link. "I thought of Gram's club the other day," she wrote, "and look what I found!" It was a page on the Lois Club website advertising the existence of a San Francisco Bay Area chapter.

I might not have been so eager to meet the Loises if I hadn't been spending all day with the cold-eyed wraiths at General Dexterity. By comparison, hanging out with a bunch of middle-aged ladies with the same name as me sounded pretty alluring.

The meeting was held in a dark-shingled house in a twisty neighborhood reached by a hidden staircase that wandered up from Parnassus Avenue. I hiked from the Farnsworth Steps to Edgewood Avenue to a cul-de-sac that backed up against the eucalyptus forest that crowned the hill.

A handwritten sign on the door read: *Welcome, Lois!*

It made me smile. I could tell that whoever wrote it was very pleased with herself. Not without reason.

The house was large and deeply lived-in, all the shelves

and surfaces stacked with books and boxes, framed pictures, old greeting cards set up like tent cities. If there was a spectrum of spaces defined at one end by my barren apartment, this marked the other extreme. Every single surface told a story. A long one. With digressions.

The Loises were in the dining room open to the kitchen, five of them clustered around a long table beside a wide window that showed a panorama of the western city—Golden Gate Park, my neighborhood beyond it, the fuzzy gray bar of the ocean beyond everything. Their hair, bleached by age, glowed in the afternoon light.

If you ever wonder about the difference between Metro Detroit and the San Francisco Bay Area: compare their Lois Clubs.

The hostess, whom I thought of as Hilltop Lois, had owned her house since 1972—an impossible span. She had once run a cheese shop at the base of the hill, and her taste had not grown less discriminating; she served us the stinkiest cheese I have ever been offered at a casual gathering. Nibbling with varying degrees of enthusiasm were also:

- Compaq Lois, who had been a marketing executive at that company in its boom years. Her wrists dripped with bracelets and chunky bangles, all gold; they piled up onto her forearms. She looked like a Valkyrie queen.
- Professor Lois, who taught anthropology at the University of San Francisco. Through the window, she pointed to the spires of St. Ignatius: "I've been climbing that hill for a decade." She was lean like a goat.
- Impeccable Lois, who possessed the kind of sartorial style that stops you on the street. She was wearing

jodhpurs—with confidence—and above them an inky denim jacket that any of the cold-eyed wraiths would have killed her to acquire. Literally murdered her. "Don't wear that down by the ballpark," I warned.

• Old Lois, who deserved a better nickname, but truly: she was old. Somewhere past ninety. Physically she seemed barely there, curled into herself, but her eyes were bright, and when I walked into the dining room and introduced myself, she crowed: "I didn't know they were still making Loises!"

They were interesting and lively, their relationships worn-in and comfortable. They had been gathering for two decades. I sat and listened and smiled and genuinely enjoyed myself, though afterward, as I padded down the Farnsworth Steps, I worried that I'd been too quiet—too boring. The other Loises had sharp opinions. They took up space.

They reminded me of Grandma Lois, and I thought about her Chicago Prison Loaf. The absurd density of it. It was the single culinary tradition my family possessed, and it was horrible.

But she had baked it all the time.

As I walked through Golden Gate Park, it struck me: the mystery of that woman's life. I hadn't ever known her, not really. I sucked in a deep breath. She had relocated from Wisconsin to Michigan, but before that she'd lived in Chicago and performed with an experimental-theater company, bunking with three other women in a tiny apartment, and not only baking that awful bread but bringing it home to share, because it was free and more or less nutritious. In later years, when she baked Chicago Prison Loaf, it must have conjured that other place, that other time. Four women in bunk beds. Midnight shows. Crimson wigs.

I sat at a computer twelve hours a day and slurped nutritive gel for lunch and dinner.

After my success in college, my neat acquisition of a job, and my precocious home purchase, I had considered myself a child of whom parents and grandparents could be proud. But it struck me then: the starkness of my apartment. Of my life. Grandma Lois, if she could have come to visit—and for the first time ever, I felt a pang, a deep wish that she could visit me here, just her alone, alive—if she could have, and if she had seen me here in San Francisco, she wouldn't have been proud of me. She would have been sad, and maybe a little bit worried.

I needed a more interesting life.

I could start by learning something.

I could start with the starter.

JESUS CHRIST IN AN ENGLISH MUFFIN

I WALKED TO THE BRIGHT BOOKSTORE on Clement Street and obtained a used copy of *The Soul of Sourdough*, written by a baker named Everett Broom, whose forearms graced the cover, taut and darkly gleaming, cradling a loaf of bread that was likewise burnished.

The book's introduction ran for twenty-two pages. It was a baker's bildungsroman, chronicling Broom's youth in Sacramento, his visits to his grandfather's bakery, his flameout as a professional skateboarder, his addiction to a home-cooked drug known as spaz rocks, and finally his retreat to a bread-baking shack on the beach and his reformation there. There were photos, all monochrome: a young man with a thick black beard below a face so clean and cherubic it made the beard appear glued on. In a photo spread across two pages, he leaned against a homemade brick oven, for which the adjective *rustic* was a favor; it looked like a pile of rubble. Scattered in the foreground were various signifiers of bohemian tranquility: a guitar, a surfboard, a book with VOLTAIRE on the spine.

He was out there learning, in his words, "to bake without

dry yeast, without desiccation, without death." Well, sure. Nobody wants death bread. Instead, he sought the alchemy of sourdough: "Wet, living, fragile, sensual. The funk of life. I smelled it on the beach, and in the forest glades where I gathered mushrooms, and in the embrace of Lucia, who was at that time my lover. And I smelled it in my starter, too."

After twenty-two pages of funk versus death, the painstaking construction from found materials of his oven, the hollow of Lucia's clavicle, et cetera, Broom figured it out. A photo showed a very young man with a very large beard grinning manically into the camera, hoisting a loaf of bread in the air like a trophy. The loaf was as big around as his chest, and, to be fair, it looked totally awesome.

He came to San Francisco, where he opened Boulangerie Broom—now a chain with three locations—and wrote this book. He shaved his beard and traded the shack for a house in Noe Valley. He married a product manager named Olivia and had two kids.

End of introduction. Next, Broom got down to business.

Sourdough bread begins with sourdough starter, which is not merely living but seething. It is a community of organisms comprised of, at minimum, yeast, which is a fungus, and lactobacillus, a bacteria. They eat flour—its sugars—and poop out acid—thus, sour—in addition to carbon dioxide, which, trapped by stretchy, glutenous dough, gives the bread an airy structure, the so-called crumb, at its prettiest a dazzling network of gaps and chambers.

Broom's first chapter described the capture and cultivation of a wild sourdough starter, a process that could take a week or more. I already possessed the Clement Street starter, so I skipped ahead.

Broom lamented the fact that we, his readers, could not bake with the benefit of a beachside shack or a rough-hewn brick oven or an Argentine lover. But he said we could still make a pretty good attempt at it, and he listed the equipment we would need:

- A digital scale, to weigh the ingredients
- A bench knife, to scrape and divide the dough
- A bread blade, to score the loaf (with a baker's mark that, ideally, matched our wrist tattoo)
- A baking stone, to absorb and emit heat in a loose simulation of Broom's brick oven (though he counseled that there was, in fact, no substitute and that, basically, he pitied us)

I opened my laptop, called up the website of an expedient internet retailer, and pecked in the name of the scale—the precise brand and model that Broom recommended. The site immediately responded: CUSTOMERS WHO BOUGHT THIS ITEM ALSO BOUGHT . . . followed by the bench knife. And the bread blade. The baking stone. King Arthur flour and Diamond Crystal salt, just as Everett Broom recommended. And finally, Broom's book itself.

The internet: always proving that you're not quite as special as you suspected.

Two days later, a UPS driver delivered the tools and ingredients to my apartment. She also delivered one apron that I had purchased from a different internet retailer, a craftier one. The apron was squarish, made from heavy denim. It looked like something a blacksmith might wear. It was the first apron I'd ever owned. I loved it.

I set out my tools. I donned my apron. Everything was in order, and I was ready to produce a beautiful, burnished loaf just like Broom's on the cover of his book.

There were detailed instructions. I love detailed instructions. My whole career was detailed instructions. Precisely specified actions, executed in order. A serene confidence settled over me.

I mixed the ingredients together, and immediately the project collapsed into chaos and disaster.

Where the bread book showed a lump of dough folded elegantly into itself, I looked upon a twisted mutant mass.

Where the bread book showed Everett Broom's clean fingers deftly maneuvering said lump, my hands soon wore thick gauntlets of glop. I waved them over the sink, tried to shake some of it loose.

Where the bread book showed a rustic work surface smartly maintained, I looked upon a cramped and dingy countertop filmed with slime.

There was dough on the cupboards. Dough on the faucet. Dough on the floor. It looked like the scene of a glutenous murder committed by a careless killer.

With each step, reality diverged further from the shining ideal pictured in the bread book, and by the end of it, I wasn't even following Broom's directions anymore, just doing whatever I could to keep the dough in one piece. It was too wet, so I added flour, then it was too dry, so I added water, and it became gloppy again, so more flour was required, and the dough grew and grew, bloblike.

There was a malevolence to it. It was not on my side.

Broom's directions indicated that it was now time to retreat while the starter did its work to make the loaf ferment and rise, and I did this gratefully. I washed my hands, tore off the apron, set the oven to preheat, opened an Anchor Steam, and flopped down in my living room. I found my laptop and set Chaiman's CD to playing. I knew every song. I'd heard them all, waiting on hold night after night.

When the timer beeped, I discovered that the dough had indeed expanded in size, and it had also firmed up somewhat. Its skin was soft but not gloppy. Glossy. I quickly folded it over onto itself, opened the oven—which was really very hot inside; was this safe? Were you truly supposed to set the temperature this high?—and dropped it onto the baking stone. Then I pushed the oven's rack back into place and slammed the door, just as a warden might slam the door on a prisoner, supremely evil and objectively irredeemable, banishing him to solitary confinement forever.

I set the oven's timer, opened another Anchor Steam, and played Chaiman's CD again. It had seven tracks, each almost ten minutes long. The music of the Mazg was entirely a cappella—a tight cluster of voices. Their language sounded Slavic, but every so often there was a hard stop, like the hitch of a sob, or an ear-bending slide between notes that spun the sound into some other, more distant dimension.

I wondered if the brothers had arrived at their destination. I thought about emailing Beoreg, but I didn't know what I would say. Our relationship had been constrained entirely by the menu. If not "Double spicy, please," then what?

FORTY MINUTES, four songs, and three beers later, the timer beeped. I opened the oven door and pulled out the rack to assess the damage.

Against all odds, the malevolent loaf emerged from the oven round and buoyant, its crust split by deep fissures. It was perhaps not as perfectly photogenic as the one on the cover of the bread book, but it was . . . not too bad.

In my exasperation, I had skipped one of Broom's steps, the one where he exhorted you to carve a baker's mark, some symbol of your own choosing. (His mark was a heart with an X through it, which was also the logo of Boulangerie Broom, seen on T-shirts and tote bags throughout San Francisco.) I had not signed my sloppy work, but there was nevertheless a clearly defined shape in the cracks and whorls of the crust.

You couldn't not see it.

The loaf had a face.

It was an illusion, of course. Jesus Christ in an English muffin. It's called pareidolia. Humans see faces in everything. Even so, the illusion was . . . compelling. This face was long and twisted, wide-eyed and openmouthed, Edvard Munch–like. Where the crust cracked, it formed furrows in the face's brow, lines around its howling mouth.

I reached down with oven mitts and lifted the loaf from the baking stone, almost expecting the face to relax in relief. Its expression remained fixed, because it was, of course, not a face but a crispy crust. I plopped it down on the countertop, fished out my phone, and snapped a picture. I was about to send it to Arjun, but something made me pause. There was real pain in the phantom face. It wasn't funny. It was disturbing. I deleted the photo.

In the bread book, Broom counseled that it was essential now to wait, to let the bread cool, to allow the glutens to complete their final binding, but I was hungry and I didn't want to stare at the face any longer. With my bread knife (which CUSTOMERS WHO BOUGHT THIS ITEM ALSO BOUGHT), I sawed through the loaf at its widest point and, like a vision in the clouds twisting apart in the wind, the illusion broke. I looked at the bread's cross section, the crumb, and I giggled a little. It didn't look like the pictures in the book; this sourdough was not so perfectly inflated, its bubbles not so lacy. But, seriously . . . not too bad!

I made another cut, peeled away a rough slice, and blew across its surface, tossing it from one hand to the other. It was too hot to eat, but I began to eat it anyway, and it tasted just like the bread that came with the double spicy.

This was Beoreg's sourdough. There was no disputing it. But as I took one mincing bite after another—I'd been waiting hours—the fact asserted itself: I'd made it myself, from nothing but flour and water and salt and a dollop of the Clement Street starter. The net cost of ingredients couldn't have been more than a dollar, and now I had this enormous loaf of bread, my favorite bread, my serenity bread. I was disappointed not to have any spicy soup for sopping. I didn't even have any butter. I ate it plain.

That loaf of bread was the first thing I'd ever prepared myself that did not come out of a box with instructions printed on the side. My apartment was suffused with its smell, the smell I knew and loved. I wanted to fish out my phone and dial the old number and cry out to Beoreg before he could put me on hold: *I did it!*

Instead, I wrote an email. Just a short message—*Look what your number one eater made!*—dispatched to the address he'd written on the menu, to which I attached a photo of myself, proudly holding up a sliver of a slice of sourdough, my cheeks full of the rest. Was it cute? It was cute. I sent it.

The twisted face in the crust was forgotten as I carved and ate, carved and ate, until the whole loaf was gone.

SHARING THE MIRACLE

THE NEXT MORNING it felt like it had been a dream, but there was the mess I'd left on the countertop, and there was the aroma, still lingering: evidence of the work I'd done, the thing I'd produced. I emailed Peter at General Dexterity to invoke one of my theoretical vacation days—I could almost hear his gasp across the city—then switched my phone to airplane mode and baked two more loaves.

This time, the dough was not so gloppy, the process not such a disaster. I waited serenely, watching three episodes of the dark serial drama while the dough fermented and rose, and another episode while the twin loaves baked.

But when I opened the oven door and pulled out the rack, I had to suck in a sharp breath. My first thought was: *You have had a tiny stroke. Possibly stress-related.* I'd read about neurological conditions that made it so you couldn't recognize people's faces; was I suffering from the opposite? Some sort of hyper-recognition? I looked around the kitchen, fixed my gaze on random objects: Cupboard. Faucet. Refrigerator. Did I see faces? I did not see faces. The power outlet looked like a little dude, but power outlets always look like little dudes.

I looked down again at the loaves on the baking stone, which, just as before, carried in their crusts the overwhelming illusion of dark eyes, upturned noses, fissured mouths.

Upon closer inspection, these faces were different from the last loaf's. They weren't disturbing. Their eyes squinted merrily and their mouths curled into ragged, jack-o'-lantern grins.

The bread knife was the solution to all my problems. I sawed and sawed until the faces were no more.

IT'S ALWAYS NEW AND ASTONISHING when it's yours. Infatuation; sex; card tricks. How many humans have baked how many loaves of bread, across how many centuries? I'm sure Beoreg baked calmly, matter-of-factly, without paroxysms of cosmic delight. But that didn't matter. For me, the novice, the miracle was intact, and I felt compelled by some force—new to me, thrillingly implacable—to share. I tied the sliced loaves into neat bundles with twine and bounded outside, still wearing the sweatpants I'd slept in.

My apartment was the lower of two units carved out of a dingy house on Cabrillo Street. My neighbor Cornelia lived upstairs. Our front doors were side by side on the face of the house, and I knocked on Cornelia's now. We didn't see each other that often, so when she appeared, her expression was cautiously curious.

I presented the twine-wrapped loaf and explained: "I . . . baked this for you?" Had I really? Was it possible? Did the universe permit feats of such profound creative alchemy? Apparently, it did.

Cornelia was, if not quite as impressed with me as I was, still at least medium-impressed. "What a nice surprise," she said, accepting the gift, and lifted it to her nose, murmuring "Mmm" appreciatively, which is exactly the right thing to do when someone presents you with the second loaf of sourdough they've ever baked in all of history.

"I didn't know you were a baker," Cornelia said.

I told her I had not been until yesterday. She raised an eyebrow, seemed to reappraise the loaf in her hands; her impressed-ness modulated upward a degree.

There was still another loaf to share. I went to the house next door, its resident unknown, never before seen or even considered. No one was home—or they were, but they were spooked by the appearance of a wild-eyed woman in sweatpants alive to the miracles of the universe, cradling a mysterious bundle, with traces of dough drying on the front of her tech company T-shirt.

The next building, then. There were three doors, and I rang the bell attached to the first. A man came to the door, flabby and whiskered, a bit drowsy looking. Behind him, deeper in his apartment, I saw a television paused on a frame of a movie; from the color palette and aspect ratio, I guessed early 2000s superhero.

"Hello," I said. "I live down the street. I was baking. I made too much." I held out the loaf.

He looked skeptical. "Nah, thanks. That's okay."

I wanted him so badly to take it. "I used the starter from Clement Street Soup and Sourdough. Did you ever order from them? Two brothers? Double spicy?"

The movie-watcher shook his head slowly, and the muscles under his eyes were wary. "Sorry. I've got to go." He closed the door, and I heard one, two, three latches click into place.

If I wanted to share this miracle—and I did—it would have to be with people who knew me.

AT THE SLURRY TABLE, when I unveiled my gift, Peter scooched his chair back apprehensively. "I don't eat bread," he reminded us. He said it like a ward against evil.

The other Slurry slurpers had no such compunctions. The slices I had sawed were thick and fluffy, and we slathered them with plum jam swiped from Chef Kate's fancy toast station.

Garrett relished the sourdough most of all. The sounds he made were borderline NSFW.

"You *made* this?" he said, mouth agape. "Like, from a kit? Does it come frozen?"

Garrett lived in one of the new micro-cube apartment buildings on Sansome Street, and his living space didn't have any kind of kitchen. Instead, it offered a wall-mounted touch screen connected to various delivery services expedited to sub-five-minute timescales through a contract with the building's owner. Garrett operated at a level of abstraction from food that made me look like Ina Garten.

I explained the process by which living sourdough starter gave the bread its texture and flavor. Garrett's eyes were wide with disbelief. "It was . . . alive," he said softly. Wonderingly. He, like me, had never before considered where bread came from, or why it looked the way it did. This was us, our time and place: we could wrestle sophisticated robots into submission, but were confounded by the most basic processes of life.

Chef Kate was making the rounds, chatting amiably with her lunchers. Generally, when she did this she avoided our table, reticent to confront the disgustingness of our food preferences. Today, Arjun called out to her—"Chef Kate!"—and she changed her course to approach us, her gaze darkening.

"Lois bakes bread now," Arjun announced.

"I didn't think you kids ate solid food," Kate said.

"That's only Peter."

"Correct," Peter said.

"Well," Kate said. "Can I try some?"

All gazes swiveled to Garrett, who had just consumed the last slice. He looked guilty but in no way repentant.

Chef Kate hooted. "I never thought I would see the day. One of the Slurry kids baking bread. The rest eating it. *Dude*." Her "dude" was a thumping approval. "Lois? Bring me some. I want to taste your wares."

THAT NIGHT, when I returned home: a new disaster.

The Clement Street starter had dried out. It was now less a slime and more a crust on the walls of the crock. Its surface was dark and rippled. It smelled like nail polish remover. It looked dead.

In a panic, I threw together a batch of the flour-water starter food. It felt like I ought to drip it in slowly, just a bit at a time, as if I were bottle-feeding an ailing kitten. (I have never bottle-fed an ailing kitten.) (I did once coax Kubrick back to life with a spray bottle.) (You have to work pretty hard to push a cactus to the brink of death.) I dripped, dripped,

48

dripped the floury paste into the crock, and as I did, I spoke to the starter.

"Come on," I murmured. "It was just one day. You're supposed to be able to handle that. The bread book said I could leave you alone for a week."

You must play the music of the Mazg, Chaiman had said. I set his CD to playing on my laptop and tapped a key to increase its volume—*plink-plink-plink.* As I fed and coddled the starter, it began to perk up. Its color lightened. One tentative bubble formed on its surface.

Relief. But also exasperation: Beoreg and Chaiman had gifted me with a starter that was strange and potent, and also extremely high-maintenance.

I left the starter to recuperate and fished from the cupboard a bottle of pinot noir (purchased for the hedgehog on its label), then retreated into my living room to sit with my eyes closed, sipping. The wine tasted vaguely like dirt. Not in a bad way. When Chaiman's CD ended, I poured the last of the wine into my glass, then played it again.

The CD's seven songs were slow and meandering and seemed to fade one into the other. Some were sung by groups of women, others by groups of men, and one was a mixed chorus. The style was all the same: sad, so very sad, but matter-of-factly so. These songs did not blubber. They calmly asserted that life was tragic, but at least there was wine in it.

I realized suddenly that my apartment reeked of bananas. I followed the scent to the kitchen, where the Clement Street starter had more than doubled in volume and was surging out of the crock, puffy tendrils oozing down the green ceramic. I heard a crispy, crackling *pock-pock-pock*; the starter was not merely bubbling but frothing.

It is only barely anthropomorphization to say it looked happy.

I could understand that.

I retired to my bedroom, where I kicked off my pants and flopped down onto my futon. I was drunk and tired and happy. More than happy: delighted. Proud of myself—not just for making the bread, but for sharing it, and for making a few friends, even if they were all programmers and Loises. Maybe programmers and Loises are all you need.

I WAS MIDWAY TO SLEEP when I heard a sound in my apartment—a whispering creak, like the bending of a board. It sounded again, louder. A dose of danger-chemicals flooded into my blood and I snapped wide-awake, eyes sharp, nose flaring.

I think some people call out "Hello?" when they hear strange sounds in the night; this has always seemed foolish to me. If the strange sound does indeed emanate from something fearful, then it already has the drop on you. Better to stay quiet; better to even the odds. I hopped up onto the balls of my feet, crept to the doorframe, slowed my breathing, and stretched my senses to listen.

The sound continued. It was less a creaking and more a high back-of-the-throat sound. *Mmm-mmm-mmm.* My pulse was throbbing in my neck.

I peeked out into the main room. My eyes flicked from the front door to the back window. Everything was shut tight. This is one virtue of a small domain: you can survey it all at once.

The sound was resolving into something residential, but

I still didn't know what. The wind whistling through a crack somewhere? I relaxed and padded out to investigate.

I followed my ears into the kitchen, where the sound was louder. Up to the countertop; louder still. I zeroed in on the source: the Clement Street starter in its crock.

As I watched, the surface of the starter trembled. It had become smooth and glossy in the moonlight.

It went, *Mmm-mmm-mmm.*

Even up close, the sound was faint. I leaned my face in, trying to discern its source. Was the crock itself flexing as it cooled in the night? Was the sound coming from a pipe behind the wall? I lifted my hand to move the crock so I could find out if the sound moved with it, and just as my fingers touched the ceramic, the *Mmm-mmm-mmm* rose and became a coherent note, then two, then more, soft but clear.

The starter was singing.

Its surface was vibrating like a pot just before boiling. This cold-simmering substance was somehow sustaining a quavering harmony.

It was singing in the key of Chaiman's CD, the key of the choirs of the Mazg.

It crooned into the darkness, then faded.

There was a silence in which I processed the fact that this crock of gray slime had been singing; in which it followed its performance with a tidy farting noise; in which it settled into quiescence; in which I moved first my fingers and then myself away from the crock, across the room, to stand against the far wall.

I wish I could say the moment was hazy or dreamlike, but I was sharp with the battle-readiness familiar to all humans of all eras awoken by strange noises in the night.

I approached the crock again, peered inside, and whispered, "Hello?"

The starter's surface had lost its shiny tautness. It sang no more.

I considered the possibilities. An accident of gas could, I reasoned, produce a sound—boiling pots bubbled merrily—but it would be plosive. It would go *pop, poof,* or *plop.* Possibly *boof* or *bloop.* Maybe—*maybe*—*ffft* or *frap*; a farting sound could be explained. I let my tongue and vocal cords go slack, forced air out of my lungs, and simulated these airy sounds. *Boof. Plop.*

But the starter had not gone *boof* or *plop.* It had murmured *Mmm-mmm-mmm* in a clear, coherent voice. You needed lips to make *Mmm,* you needed a brain to find a note. That was complicated equipment.

I looked down at the Clement Street starter. It was not complicated.

I set the crock's lid in place and padded back to bed. Sleep came slowly.

IT'S A MESS when strange events smack into the windscreen of a resolutely rational mind. It would have been tidy to believe that it was a ghost speaking to me through the malleable medium of goopy dough. There's a whole story there: I could have organized a séance, hired a specialized kitchen exorcist, et cetera. But, of course, I do not believe in kitchen ghosts, or sourdough angels, or 500-degree devils, and so the event I had witnessed had to be explained by actually existing physical and/or mental phenomena. I simply could not come up with any.

The next day was Saturday, and I spent most of it trying to devise a way in which the starter's song might have been a bit of dream shifted into waking—the mental equivalent of an off-by-one error. But the sound was sharp in my memory.

I ejected Chaiman's CD and turned it over in my hands. Its title was handwritten. There was no label, no publisher, no bar code. There were no clues.

I opened my laptop and searched in vain for information on world writing systems. I found a comparative table of scripts, but at the top of the page it warned that there were thousands of written languages on Earth, some of them with just a handful of writers, and it would be impossible to list them all. Nothing in the table matched the script on the CD, the script on Beoreg's menu.

I'd received no reply to my email.

The starter did not sing that day. It did not evince any special glossiness. It did not respond to questioning. I didn't try to bake. Instead, I watched it closely, stirred it with a spoon, stuck my nose into the crock. It was mute, though fragrant.

Bananas.

CHEF KATE

O N MONDAY, I rose early and baked two loaves that emerged from the oven with faces happy-cheeked, cherubic. I wrapped them in paper towels and stuffed them into my backpack.

I also carried the crock with its fragile passenger along to the office and set it on my desk next to Kubrick the cactus. I threaded a pair of earbuds between my laptop and the crock, dangled them inside, and played Chaiman's CD at minimum volume.

The cafeteria was nearly empty, with only a few early risers (or never-slepters), who sat quietly with code and yogurt. In the kitchen, Chef Kate and her small staff were subdividing a pile of potatoes, collecting tater-tot-sized pieces in plastic tubs. Reggae played on a whoomphy Bluetooth speaker.

Chef Kate had come to oversee the feeding of the Dextrous by way of a cool restaurant on Valencia Street, wooed away from fine dining by lavish stock options and normal work hours. For Andrei, she was a trophy. His chowhound ways were well-known, as was his dream of seeing his robot arms working smoothly alongside sous chefs in all the open kitchens of the city.

I lifted my swaddled loaves in greeting. Chef Kate cleared a space among the potatoes.

She brought a loaf to her nose, then thunked its backside with her finger and listened to the report. "Very nice." She produced a serrated blade and commanded me to cut while she stepped away in search of something else.

Once every quarter, Andrei insisted that Chef Kate employ the robot arms in her kitchen, and once every quarter, the robot arms failed her horribly. The latest tryout sat in the corner, powered down with a broom leaned up against it, waiting to be wheeled back across the street to the Task Acquisition Center. We would solve everything else before we solved the egg problem.

I followed Kate's instructions and sawed off two rough slices. She returned with butter and salt and generously dressed both of them. "There." The bread was now blanketed with bright yellow butter. It glittered with a crust of flaky salt. It seemed excessive.

Kate hoisted her slice in a salute and said, "You'd be better off eating *this* every day than that Slurry shit." She took a bite. "Dude." Chewed. Took another bite. Said again: "Dude." Swallowed. "You could sell this."

I told her Arjun said the same thing.

"Arjun doesn't know anything. I do. This is a solid product. Dude. Sell me some."

She fixed me with a challenging gaze. This was not the empty jollity of a friend's "You could sell this"; this was the hard-eyed appraisal of someone who spent a lot of time thinking about what was and wasn't commercially viable.

This was, in other words, a real offer.

I told her okay. I would sell her some.

"What's your capacity?"

"Not much? I can bake two loaves in my oven. So I can do four, I guess, in a couple of hours."

"I need at least eight. You kids eat a lot."

I told her I would find a way to do eight. I had no idea how, but that's what I told her.

"Bring them next week," Chef Kate said. "Trial run, Monday through Friday. Cool?"

Cool, I agreed, and I could not account fully for the thrill of the prospect. Maybe it was the miracle of baking, still alive for me; maybe it was the fact that I'd never produced anything that earned such a visceral reaction before. Visceral was nice. Visceral was fun.

"I pay Everett Broom five dollars a unit, which is absurd, but I'll pay you the same, on the strength of this loaf. Thirty days net. Bring me an invoice."

Units! Net! Invoices! I was drunk with it.

"See you next Monday," Chef Kate said. "Early!"

Back at my desk, I sat smiling—grinning goofily, in fact— and wondered if it was the first time I had ever done so sitting at that desk. The Clement Street starter was happy, too— burbling merrily—and my workspace was permeated by the faint smell of bananas and the croon, even fainter, of the choirs of the Mazg, whoever they were.

HELLO, NUMBER ONE EATER! Your sourdough looks splendid. I'm very happy to see it. Does it smell like bananas—just a tiny bit?

Chaiman and I are back in Edinburgh, crowded into Shehrieh's small apartment here. (That's my mother. Mazg don't say "Mom" and "Dad." I don't really know why not.) I'm cooking for everyone. After a year of practice in San Francisco, I think it's happened: I'm finally a better cook than my mother. She won't admit it, of course, but I can tell she's nervous. I have a batch of spicy soup going now, with an ingredient that is, wickedly, new to her: FRESNO CHILI! I discovered it on Clement Street. Yes, I think this is going to be the night she concedes. Please picture me rubbing my hands together like a villain.

Send more messages!

THE JAY STEVE VALUE OVEN

THE CHALLENGE from Chef Kate smoldered in my brain. It was a familiar burn. I broke down the tolerances, the timings. To produce bread in the quantity she required, I would either have to start at three in the morning and bake loaves two at a time for four hours . . . or I would have to acquire a bigger oven.

Midway through *The Soul of Sourdough*, in a sidebar, Everett Broom alluded to the deep satisfaction of building a brick oven of one's own. "A full exploration of the design considerations is beyond the scope of this book," he wrote, "but you'll find a helpful community online at Global Gluten."

Global Gluten turned out to be a collection of forums populated by a kind of person I hadn't known existed: the carbohydrate nerd. They talked about hydration ratios, pH levels, dough temperatures. They traded recipes and swapped starters.

And, as Broom had promised, they gathered in a subforum devoted to the design and construction of elaborate wood-fired brick ovens. Here, the carb nerds shared blueprints.

The ovens they built were beautiful, architectural, like miniature Byzantine churches. For each design, there was a corresponding "heat curve" that swelled to 800 degrees or more, then eased down slowly for hours. The carb nerds got very, very excited about the shapes of these curves.

There were a few message threads pinned to the top of the forum—perennial references. One of them had been created six years ago and boasted seventy-nine pages of commentary. Its title was: THE JAY STEVE $200 VALUE OVEN (VERSION SIX).

I investigated. There were pictures, captured in a backyard that presumably belonged to Jay Steve. The grass was brown and patchy. There was a chain-link fence and a plastic dog dish.

And there was an oven, neither Byzantine nor beautiful. Instead, it was fully *Mad Max*: a squarish jumble of brick and metal. If I'd stumbled across the picture in a different context I would have assumed I was looking at the remains of a very small shanty following a great conflagration. The lines were askew; the metal was rusted; the bricks around the door were stained black with char.

Following Jay Steve's initial post (his profile picture was the affable snout of a golden retriever) were the seventy-nine pages of comments in which the carb nerds proposed tweaks of all kinds—different dimensions, different materials—but at some point all conceded: this was a badass little oven.

I could acquire all the materials at the expedient big-box home-supply store. Unfortunately, my car was minuscule and its tiny engine moaned even when it was carrying just me and zero home supplies over San Francisco's hills. I knocked on my upstairs neighbor's door, and when Cornelia appeared, I asked her if I could borrow her car.

"Nobody drives it but me," she said. "You need to go somewhere? I'll drive you. What day is it? Yeah. I should get out."

Cornelia's car was her defining feature. I saw it approximately a hundred times more often than I saw her: a battered green Honda CR-V that was always parked directly in front of the house, except for when Cornelia was working, when she replaced it with four traffic cones. As I watched, she removed them from the trunk and plunked them down.

The car's windshield was bordered with the badges and shields of every extant on-demand delivery service, along with several that were now defunct. While she navigated us to the expedient big-box home-supply store just south of the city, she swiped through a long carousel of apps with one hand and, I sensed, ninety percent of her attention. "Nah," she murmured. "Nah. Nah. Nah."

Cornelia was a highly strategic pawn in the on-demand delivery marketplace. Most hours of most days, she lounged at home in her sweatpants. But she was at all times monitoring the apps, and at the moments when demand burned blue-hot—Friday nights, often, but also random Tuesdays when the fog was at its thickest, suggesting to people that they ought to stay home and ponder their lives over delivered Burmese food—Cornelia would spring into action and earn a thousand dollars in a tire-screeching rally worthy of *Bullitt*. When it rained, she paid her rent in a day.

At the expedient big-box home-supply store, I wound my way through the towering aisles, following the shopping list provided by Jay Steve. I amassed thirty-six cinder blocks; two hundred and twenty-six plain red bricks (not firebricks, which Jay Steve claimed were for "luxury ovens only"); one bag each of clay and sand; one two-by-four cut to measure; and a supply of kindling, which the store sold in neat boxes.

When I returned to the car with three polo-shirted helpers pushing three different carts laden with materials, the trunk of Cornelia's CR-V was already open and she was perched on the bumper, swiping through her phone, wearing a satisfied, catlike look. While I had shopped, she had completed two delivery missions, earning fifty dollars.

She ferried me and my materials back to Cabrillo Street, the CR-V riding noticeably lower to the ground, and there we hauled my acquisitions one by one around the side of the building into a heap in the backyard.

"What are you doing out here?" Cornelia huffed at last.

I told her, with as much confidence as I could muster, that I was constructing a wood-fired brick oven in our backyard.

"How . . . crafty."

She retreated to the front of our building. I considered its bulk. It was charmless, a blank expanse of stubbly pseudo-stucco broken by just two windows: mine at eye level, Cornelia's above. The appropriate next step in this project would have been to contact the property management company, explain what I wanted to do, perhaps offer to increase my security deposit by some as-yet-unknown amount, and hope for official assent.

It was early evening.

The sky was a low ceiling of fog.

I shooed away the Cabrillo Street cats.

I beat back the weeds.

I built the oven.

It was shockingly easy because the instructions had been refined by Global Gluten's collective cleverness into something approaching IKEA-grade ease, and also because it was just a box. A box for fire.

I stacked the cinder blocks to mid-thigh, forming the oven's base. Then I assembled its floor and walls and ceiling, three bricks thick all around, leaving a gap a few bricks wide for the door. Finally, I mixed the clay and sand with water to make a mortar that I slathered into the cracks between bricks. I did this with my bare hands, as Jay Steve recommended. Whatever mortar remained I painted onto the oven's top and sides.

The bricks were the crux of it, Jay Steve explained. Prior to this just-in-time education, I had assumed that in a wood-fired brick oven, the flames of the fire baked the bread. I mean, of course, right? Wrong. Baking in this oven would be a two-step process, and the first was for the fire to charge those thick walls with heat. The thicker the walls, the more heat they could absorb and then return. In an oven like this, it was the bricks, not the fire, that baked the bread.

My oven looked like a gloppy cube, without even the crudest approximation of the graceful heat-reflecting domes that topped the fancier designs. But Jay Steve was insistent: *Ugly ovens bake great bread.*

The crowning touch was the door, a plug of thick wood built from the two-by-four cut to measure.

The sun had set. Fog was rolling into the yard, cold and dense. The oven was done. I stepped back to appraise it. It looked like a pile of junk. It was a success.

I wanted badly to try it out, but here, Jay Steve cautioned, impatience spelled doom. Before I could bake with it, I had to cure the oven by building a very small fire, then growing it larger, and larger still, all over the course of several hours, until I had reached peak flameage (about 800 degrees), and, in the process, coaxed the latent moisture out of the bricks. If I rushed the process and baked at full strength right away, the oven would crack. It would become even uglier, and, worse, it would never bake in fully badass fashion.

I pushed a few logs inside, arranged them in a loose triangle, tucked some kindling into place, and lit my first fire. It smoked and fumed. A lick of flame appeared, inspected its nest, proclaimed it satisfactory, and began to crackle.

There were four ancient lawn chairs lying in a tangle behind the recycling bin, evidence of long-departed residents, with vines growing through their seats. I ripped away the vines, carried one of the chairs to the oven, plopped it down, and sat.

I waited.

It was cold, maybe forty degrees. I dashed inside to retrieve a blanket, my jacket, and an additional sweater, and when I returned to the lawn chair, I piled them all on top of myself. I slithered one hand through the heap to grasp and manipulate my poker (a long straight stick gleaned from the back of the yard) while keeping the skin–air interface to a minimum.

I had another thought, and with reluctance I dismantled my insulating heap to go back inside and retrieve the Clement Street starter in its crock. Wary of the cold, I wedged it into the lawn chair next to me, then built the heap on top of it. I figured the starter ought to be present for the beginning of this important next phase in our work together.

On the back of the building, the upper window flickered with the movement of blinds. They snapped up and the window slid open with a sharp squeak. A Cornelia-shaped silhouette appeared. I heard a curious "Hmm" and the sil-houette retreated. A few minutes later, Cornelia emerged around the side of the building. She extricated another lawn chair, dragged it over, and plopped herself down.

"Be a shame if the management company heard about this," she said.

It would be a shame, indeed.

"You could keep your neighbor quiet pretty easy, though. Bribe her. I bet she just wants more of that bread."

Did she now.

"Mm-hmm." She leaned toward the oven, opened her palms to the heat. "Why bake it out here? Does it make a difference?"

I began to list the virtues of the Jay Steve Value Oven as I had learned them on the message board, not least of which was its capacity: for $200 of raw materials and a few hours of labor—not including these hours of fire-watching, which were decidedly unlaborious—I had doubled my baking ca-pacity. I could fit four loaves inside this oven. Four! And they would come out better. This was a wood-fired brick oven, the kind used by Everett Broom, and also by the artisan bakers of ancient days . . .

I stopped talking, and we were quiet, watching the fire burn.

After a while, Cornelia hoisted herself up with a little grunt, said good night, and padded into the building. I saw her silhouette in the window. She waved, then disappeared, and the light went out, but the window was still open to the cold night air and the smell of the fire.

I fell asleep; for how long, I wasn't sure. When I woke up, the oven was still going strong. The bricks weren't steaming and crackling anymore. The curing process was well under way.

The crock wedged next to me was vibrating with the starter's tremors of growth, even though I hadn't fed it. Was it responding to the warmth? I peeled back a sweater and the blanket and heard its quiet musing leaking out into the night.

The air was heavy and cold, and when I looked up, I saw a surprise. The oven's heat, rising in a steady plume, had bored through the fog and cleared a channel to the sky.

I saw stars.

YOU ASKED what makes the Mazg the Mazg. I've been thinking about it, and I've come up with three things.

First is our food. Most Mazg would say the culture—the starter—is the crucial thing, and of course the sourdough. Honestly . . . it's not my favorite. I like the spicy better. But I think you already knew that.

Second is our singing! Easy one.

Third is our reticence. There are Mazg neighborhoods in cities all over Europe, but you would never know it, because we never have signs or storefronts. You will never, ever see our beautiful script on the street.

It's a shame.

THE PROBLEM WAS ONGOING

I ROSE BEFORE DAWN, carried the loaves into the backyard, started a fire in the Jay Steve, let it roar. When I reached in to push the coals to the back, the intensity of the heat made it suddenly clear the oven in my kitchen was no oven at all. The tiny hairs on my arms all vaporized. Four loaves went in and I jammed the wooden plug into place. Then I did a little jig.

Forty minutes later, my hands shielded by thick mitts, I yanked the plug.

The loaves were bigger than before, colored a deeper gold. Clearly visible in the cracks and crevices of the crust were the wide smiles they wore.

Everybody was happy.

The simple math of it was astonishing, and I felt the giddy leverage of technology—more palpably, I should add, than at any moment during my General Dexterity orientation. This was simple and direct: Before the machine, I could make two loaves. After the machine, I could make four. For the first time in my life, I realized why a person might be interested in capital. This was capital!

I slammed through one batch of four loaves, then another. It took every ounce of restraint not to cut into the sourdough myself.

It wasn't even six a.m. and I had a set of loaves, rough octuplets, all smiling. I had stopped worrying about the faces. I wrapped the loaves in paper towels, resolved to buy more appropriate swaddling—what was the appropriate swaddling?— and hustled out the door.

It was still dark outside. To the east, downtown San Francisco was obscured by hills, but the lights glowed splotchy purple on the underbelly of the marine layer.

The General Dexterity office was quiet but not deserted. Chef Kate was in her kitchen, bent over a notebook, building a tall, skinny to-do list. Her two sous chefs stood at their stations, rapping their knives through thick heads of cabbage and long green onions. This morning, it was slow-rolling hip-hop on the Bluetooth speaker.

"Here's your first shipment," I said, presenting the loaves.

Chef Kate inspected them one by one. "These look pretty good," she said. "Consistent. But this—the crust." She indicated the whorls of the faces. "How the hell do you do that?"

I told her it had been an accident the first time, and I'd repeated the steps every time since, which was technically the truth, if not entirely forthright.

"It's weird, dude. But I think I like it. You got an invoice for me, or what?"

Later that day, I carried it to her, warm from the office printer. Forty dollars. I made more than that in fifteen minutes of programming, but this money felt special.

It was a decidedly different kind of work.

At General Dexterity, I was contributing to an effort to

make repetitive labor obsolete. After a trainer in the Task Acquisition Center taught an arm how to do something, all the arms did it perfectly, forever.

In other words, you solved a problem once, and then you moved on to more interesting things.

Baking, by contrast, was solving the same problem over and over again, because every time, the solution was consumed. I mean, really: chewed and digested.

Thus, the problem was ongoing.

Thus, the problem was perhaps the point.

On Tuesday morning, I baked eight more loaves.

Every day after work, rather than migrate to the bar down the street with Arjun, I went straight home. I timed the bus perfectly, ran from the stop on Fulton Street to my front door, barreled into my apartment—because I had so much to do. I had to mix fresh dough, let it sit, work it again, shape it into loaves. All before bedtime, and bedtime was early, with a bar of sunlight still crossing the foot of my futon. It felt strange but good.

Wednesday: eight more loaves.

My hours at my desk became a blur. The moment I left the office, my brain shifted gears; the interlocking complexities of ArmOS were gone, evaporated, and all that existed was the labor ahead.

Thursday: eight more loaves.

Chef Kate made grilled cheese sandwiches using my sourdough and I saw them consumed in the cafeteria. I saw roboticists' faces rapt with pleasure. I saw Andrei, the CEO, carrying one on his tray.

I took loose slices of sourdough, buttered luxuriously in the Chef Kate style, over to the Slurry table. Peter sharply declined, of course, but Arjun and Garrett both snatched them up greedily. "This is so good," Garrett said. "Can I order it online?"

Friday: eight more loaves.

Some mornings, the repetition felt Zen-like; others, Sisyphean. But in either case, it felt good to use my arms, not my fingertips. My nose, not my eyes.

On Friday afternoon, Chef Kate told me the sourdough had been "pretty freakin' good, dude"—I squealed—and asked me to keep it coming.

As I MENTIONED BEFORE, nearly every large city in Europe has a community of Mazg, but they can be hard to detect. The Mazg like to live in alleys and courtyards, or up above the street. One of my uncles calls us "the second-story people," which has a nice sound to it, I guess.

Here's the thing.

I think many of my relatives like being obscure because it means they can't be ambitious either. It lets them off the hook.

I think more people should know about the Mazg—particularly our cuisine. I think we should have restaurants with signs and front doors.

I think a lot of things.

A CATALOG OF PHENOMENA

THE RHYTHM WENT LIKE THIS: In the evening, when I got home from General Dexterity, I would play Chaiman's CD and feed the Clement Street starter. I would wait for it to bubble and grow and suffuse the apartment with its banana scent. Then I would section off half of the mass, mix it into my dough, and form the loaves, which I would set beside the open kitchen window to rise slowly overnight in the naturally occurring refrigerator that was the Richmond District.

I went to sleep, but that wasn't the end of the day for the starter. Many nights—not all, but many—it woke me with its grumblings and exhalations.

A catalog of phenomena:

- Tiny winking bubbles produced not randomly but in a perfect grid across the starter's surface, like turbines on a power plant floor
- A dusting of pinprick lights, luminous powdered sugar
- Stronger lights emanating from deeper within the starter's bulk, blurred like the sodium glow of a city

viewed from a window seat on an airplane landing in low clouds
- A fine mazelike patterning on the starter's surface, retracting into smoothness upon my approach
- Songs, various: all in the key of Chaiman's CD
- Scents, various: with banana as the backbone, always, but adding other fruity currents as well as, on one memorable night, the smell of smoke so potent I thought for a moment the Jay Steve had lit the backyard on fire

Always that glossiness; always the moment when it wasn't slime but something firmer, more self-possessed.

Always I saw these things in darkness, usually past midnight, in various states of wakefulness. Some of the encounters felt dreamlike, and in fact I suspected at least one really was a dream; others were as sharp and vivid as that first song.

When I saw the pinprick lights, I tried to snap a photo with my phone, but in the morning my camera roll was just a line of swampy rectangles, the outline of the crock barely darker than the countertop, the lights I had seen with my eyes not sufficiently bright to register pixels on the camera's sensor.

Another night, with the city-like extrusions, I tried again, this time using my phone's flash, and it bounced back brightly from the shiny ceramic crock, blinding me. A moment passed, my eyes swam pink, and then the starter, summoning some hidden energy, flashed back. It was the faintest flicker of green, but it registered like a signal flare across a vast abyss. A message from Alpha Centauri. The resulting photo was awful and alien, like the time I tried to take a picture of the inside of my mouth to check on a blister that was forming. (Sorry, but I did.)

When the starter sang, I tried to record it, but these recordings, like the pictures, were all inscrutable in the morning. Either my phone's mic didn't pick up anything, or my own ragged breathing drowned it out, or there was a note faintly audible, but so what? Who was I going to play it for? On what website was I going to post it? Global Gluten? New thread: *Does anyone else's starter sing? Here's a clip.*

I stopped getting up. The rattle of the crock's lid would rouse me, and I would listen for a minute, then roll over and go back to sleep.

AT THE CLOSE OF THE THIRD WEEK, Chef Kate summoned me to her kitchen.

"So, I love this bread, but these kids can't tell the difference, and it's bumming me out." She waved her hand dismissively at the cafeteria.

I felt a twinge of shame. Was this Chef Kate's life? Preparing great food for a terminally unappreciative clientele? No one ever ate the creative salads. Meanwhile, the tater tots were depleted in minutes.

"It's really special," Kate said. "You know that, right?"

I had suspected it, but hearing her say it plucked a string inside me.

"I think you should try to get a spot at a farmers market. The faces in the crust, they're weird. People like that shit. Do you know how the markets work? No, of course you don't. There's an audition every month. Fancy judges. Mostly insufferable, but Lily Belasco is okay. If they like what you bring, they assign you to a market. Lake Merritt, if you're

74

lucky. Colma, if you're not. I'm pretty sure you'll get a spot if you try."

I told her I would think about it, and she was quiet a moment.

"I'm sure you like your work here," Kate said. "I have no idea what you do. No, please don't try to explain it. But I feel like I have to tell you, for what it's worth . . . feeding people is really freakin' great. There's nothing better."

Even feeding people as ungrateful as the Dextrous?

She began to reply, but something caught her eye, and instead she shouted to one of her sous chefs: "*Mario! We need a bacon refresh!*" She turned back to me. "Trust me, if I could pay for my kid's school with farmers market dollars, I'd be there right alongside you."

THE LOIS CLUB (CONTINUED)

I MESSAGED HILLTOP LOIS and told her I would bring bread to the next meeting of the Lois Club.

I'm so glad you're coming back!! she replied. *We were afraid we might have scared you off. Flashy Lois can be a bit much . . .*

It was nice to know we each had our own system for Lois disambiguation. Who was I to them? Young Lois, I supposed. Better than Boring Lois, or Lois Whose Stomach Hurt.

In fact, my stomach had been feeling pretty good lately.

So it came to pass that the Loises of the San Francisco Bay Area built open-faced sandwiches, piling prosciutto and fig over soft slathers of goat cheese all atop slices of my bread. They ate all of it, every crumb, and they oohed their appreciation.

"I've been baking bread for twenty years," Professor Lois said, "and it never turned out this good."

"My starter is unique," I said.

She snorted. "I get mine in the mail from King Arthur—the flour company. Every three months it dies and I order a new one."

The Loises shared their updates. Compaq Lois was organizing a fund-raiser for a turkey vulture research center; Professor Lois had just returned from an academic conference in Montreal; Impeccable Lois would soon acquire a vintage Moog synthesizer for a very good price; and Old Lois was still alive.

I told the Loises about my baking adventures—they interrupted to say, "It's really great," and "Truly, Lois, dear, you have a gift"—and also about Chef Kate's challenge.

"I love the farmers markets," Professor Lois cooed. "You should do it." The other Loises nodded in agreement.

Compaq Lois spoke. Her voice was not kind or coddling, but stern. "Do you like your job?"

My hesitation answered for me.

"I know I have strong opinions about everything—I can't help it, I do—but this one's the strongest. I waited too long to get out of that office. Much too long. I weep for those years."

The seriousness of her statement quieted the room.

"If this is fun for you—and I think it is fun for you? Damn, you're good at it. You should try out for those markets. See what happens."

The other Loises murmured their assent. Everyone wore inward looks, perhaps contemplating the things they wished they'd done sooner.

"Thanks," I said. "I appreciate the advice."

The wine was gone, so Hilltop Lois, wearing a mischievous look, uncorked a bottle of port. I got the sense this did not happen at every meeting of the Lois Club, but the ones at which it did: those were the good ones.

"I envy you, Lois the Younger," sighed Compaq Lois.

"No, no, she's Computer Lois," said Hilltop Lois.

"We all have names? Who am I?" Old Lois interjected.

There was a pause. "You're Most Respected Elder Lois," said Impeccable Lois, who was today wearing a tweed suit tailored close to her body with pleats of intimidating sharpness.

Old Lois sniffed. "I don't like it. Anyway, I think she has to be Lois the Baker now."

"The bread was awfully good," Compaq Lois agreed. She flipped the last remaining sliver of fig into her mouth and looked at me pointedly. "See what happens," she said.

The setting sun lit the house in orange and pink and it made all the Loises look great. Emerging from the bathroom, I caught a glimpse of myself in a hallway mirror. My hair was longer than it had been in years, and it glowed in the sunset, the ends alight like burning filament. Lois the Baker looked great, too.

Cars appeared. One was from the expedient internet car service and Compaq Lois waved as she stepped in, her bracelets glittering. The other cars were piloted by various Lois associates. Professor Lois's husband read *The Atlantic* while he waited. Old Lois's daughter helped her into the passenger seat of a Toyota, laughing at some quiet joke. Impeccable Lois's girlfriend drove an old Ford pickup truck.

On top of the city with my Loises all around me, I felt a tremor of something. Was it possible?

I had become interesting.

I KEEP WRITING "the Mazg" like it's such a definite thing. In fact, Leopold (my father) is Dutch. Shehrieh's mother was Italian. Truthfully, Chaiman and I could, if we wanted, decide not to be Mazg. I have a cousin who did that. She makes dresses in Barcelona now. But Chaiman and I have . . . attachments. For me, it's the food, and for Chaiman, it's the music, and for both of us, it's Shehrieh, who is Mazg through and through, whatever that even means. We are both always trying to impress her *and* not disappoint her, which can be a tricky combination.

THE GREATEST OF ALL THE MARKETS

I'D NEVER SEEN SO MANY PICKLES in my life.

We were lined up, a hundred of us, all with our samples like offerings for a queen or a newborn prophet. Boxes and baskets and bottles and jars—so many jars: some jars plain, others with clever labels already designed and printed in anticipation of a bright future at one of the Bay Area's many markets.

Not all of those labels would be needed.

The woman in front of me was clutching a jar of Japanese pickled plums between her breasts, staring into space, moving her lips, subvocalizing. Rehearsing.

Behind me was another woman who seemed somewhat more serene. She'd brought a tall bottle of olive oil labeled with a strip of masking tape that read PICHOLINE. In a cardboard carrier, she had eight tiny blue tasting glasses shaped like tulips.

"It's amazing, isn't it?" she said, her eyes roaming the space.

The Ferry Building was more than amazing; it was mythic.

This grand structure on the city's edge, perched on pylons,

built a hundred years ago and in the middle of that century, not merely abandoned but actually walled off by a dark freeway that curled around the Embarcadero like a rampart. Then, an earthquake came and it was like something out of a fairy tale: the wall tumbles, the spell fades, and the townspeople realize what a gift they've possessed all along.

The Ferry Building was rebuilt, reopened. It was better than ever, and best of all on Saturdays, when it unfurled itself into a farmers market that filled up the plazas, reached out onto the piers. Trucks converged from a hundred miles in every direction carrying fruits, nuts, vegetables, flowers, fresh meat; the whole bounty of California. The sun glittered on the bay and the big bridge to Oakland bracketed the scene like a picture frame.

This was the greatest of all the markets, and basically no one in this line had a chance of getting a spot here. I'd learned this online, searching for information about the tryout. You started on the periphery and made your way to the bright bustling core.

It was Wednesday, so there was no market, but even during the week, the Ferry Building was a prodigious hub of gastronomical commerce. We petitioners were lined up on a catwalk above the building's main concourse, where shops sold cheese and chocolate, beef and beans, knives and cookbooks and garden gloves. Midday sunshine streamed in through skylights that ran the length of the building. Tourists and locals alike gathered around Greenlight Coffee, watching the baristas take their time.

In San Francisco, there is a particular trajectory available to food-related enterprises. Your little venture—maybe it's called Greenlight Coffee!—begins with a ramshackle cart at the outermost corner of a far-flung farmers market. Colma: market of the dead. In a year or two, having established your dedication, you are invited to the Ferry Building. This is your audition. The right person sees you—and the right person is assuredly here, canvassing the stalls—and you are springboarded, granted a small storefront in a rapidly gentrifying neighborhood. If the storefront is successful—if it assists with the greater aims of gentrification, is written up in national food and/or lifestyle publications, including, ideally, *The New York Times* (the local paper can't help you here)—then you will be permitted to open a larger, more boldly designed flagship along one of the city's Certified Cool Thoroughfares. In a few years, you will have expanded into a few additional locations, including a permanent spot in the Ferry Building—a gleaming café bathed in that midday light. You will have become a celebrated local mini-chain. Finally, you will sell your company to Starbucks for nineteen million dollars. And remember: You began with the cart at the outermost corner. You began here, in this line.

That's why I was petitioner number forty-three, with more people behind me than in front. This tryout occurred once a month. We would have had better odds applying to Stanford as adult learners.

When I reached the front of the line, a bright-eyed Ferry Building functionary explained what I was about to experience. The deal, she said, was this: Three minutes with the panel. Offer a taste; just a taste. Explain what makes you different. Be eloquent but concise but confident but deferential. Much of this is beyond your control; if you make pickles but the markets are overflowing with them, it won't matter how great your pickles are.

The woman with the Japanese pickled plums was inside now.

The loaf I had baked that morning had cooled completely, and suddenly I wished I'd carried it in some kind of insulating sleeve. But then, I supposed, it might have turned soggy. How *do* you store and transport bread? I didn't know anything. That was the absurdity of this: I was standing in line with people who were masters of their craft. People who pickled plums, pressed olives, raised chickens, kept bees. I was just lucky: gifted with good raw materials and, perhaps, charitably, a sense for how to use them.

The Clement Street starter was waiting back at my desk.

"Smells good," the functionary said, catching a whiff of the bread. I wished suddenly that I'd brought the starter itself. I wished I'd trained it to sing on command. I could have put it in front of the panel and said, *Have you ever seen anything like this?*

The functionary explained that the panel would taste my sourdough and hear my plea, then announce its market placements later in the afternoon. Placement was conditional on my willingness to sign certain agreements and also on certain logistical double checks that she, the functionary, would make. If I wasn't placed anywhere—well, most of the people in this line had been turned down many times already. You can always try again, the functionary said. You were allowed to return once a season. People applied and reapplied, groveled and waited, for years. The Greenlight Coffee people had done that. Nineteen million dollars.

The door opened. The pickler of plums emerged, her face a tangle of vexations. I tried to catch her eye, to give her an encouraging look, but she was all wrapped up in herself, carrying her jar toward the stairs that would lead her down to the main concourse, where perhaps she would acquire a cone of cardamom ice cream to assuage her anxiety.

The bright-eyed functionary held open the door to the panel's chamber and wished me good luck.

TONIGHT, CHAIMAN AND I counted through all the places we've ever lived: Brussels, Budapest, Turin, Avignon, Edinburgh, San Francisco. That's six—about average for a couple of Mazg. I don't know if I should count Edinburgh twice, now that we're back here. Chaiman's favorite city is San Francisco. ("FOR SURE," he is shouting.) I don't think I've found mine yet.

THE PANTHEON

T HE ROOM WAS WIDE and well windowed with a blinding view of the bay, Yerba Buena Island directly ahead. Seven judges sat in a line at a long table, four women and three men, swaddled and comfortable, wrapped in scarves and caftans. Plain fabrics, generous cuts. They had different-colored skin and different-colored hair, but they shared a satisfied plumpness. It looked like a committee of harvest gods drawn from all the pantheons.

All except one, seated at the end of the table, who seemed less Demeter or Dionysus, more Hades. Her hair was shiny and slicked back; she wore a slouchy black leather jacket over a shimmering black T-shirt. Maybe she was the token goddess of death, and also of street fashion.

Welcome, the gods murmured together. What do you have for us today?

They were smiling, apple-cheeked, with friendly wrinkles around their eyes. They were wide-framed and golden-whiskered. They didn't seem like cruel, uncompromising judges at all. Even the queen of the underworld was smiling.

Let's have a taste, they said.

There was a bread knife waiting in a tray alongside other knives as well as spoons and cups. The instruments of ritual. Using the Ferry Building knife, I sawed seven generous slices.

Tell us about this bread you've made, they said. We do have many bakers already. But, Jacqueline, you never know. The Inner Sunset could use a good sourdough. That's a fair point, Marco. Let her speak. Tell us about it.

"It's unique," I said. "That's why I brought it. Sourdough depends on its starter, right? This starter is special, and I thought you would appreciate it." A bit of flattery. They received it well. There was fluttering and cooing and those with whiskers stroked them.

I watched them eat. They did so carefully, all at their own pace. They sniffed the bread, flipped it over, tore it into smaller pieces. One gray-haired goddess held it up to the light, peering through the crumb of the bread as if it were a stained-glass window.

This is good, they said. Very good indeed. But we do have bread already. We have many fine sourdoughs. Is this superior? Is there a market where it fits?

A bearded god of wine and festivals asked pointedly: To what baking tradition would you say this belongs?

That stumped me. I would have been very comfortable lying, but I didn't know any baking traditions at all. I was about to say I learned from Everett Broom, but I stopped myself; every baker who walked into this chamber must have learned from Everett Broom.

"Actually, I work at a tech company," I confessed. "General Dexterity, do you . . . ? Okay, no. I served this in the cafeteria there, and Chef Kate . . . I mean, Kate . . ." I realized I didn't know her last name.

"Kate Rossi," said the goddess of the dead. "Did she send you here? That's interesting."

From beneath a luxurious beard came a gentle query: "A tech company, you said? Are you . . . technical?"

I told them I was a programmer.

"And which do you prefer? Baking . . . or programming?"

"Do I have to choose?"

You might, they said. The day may come. Lake Merritt, it's very busy, it demands everything of a vendor . . . Do you think she's right for Lake Merritt? Oh no, no no no, I was just making a point.

The central goddess, a woman wrapped in a light blue shawl, had been silent. Now she quieted the rest with the tiniest motion of her hand. She had barely nibbled the bread. There was no charity in her eyes when she looked at me and said, "That will be all."

"Okay," I said. "Thanks."

Thank you for bringing this to us, they said. Thank you for bringing yourself.

LATER, I WAS WAITING for the announcements, walking in circles around the perimeter of the Ferry Building, two licks into a cone of soothing pistachio ice cream, when a voice called out to me. "You, with the bread."

Me, with the bread?

It was the queen of the underworld. She stood in the shadow of the pillars that supported the Ferry Building's great roof, smoking a cigarette, looking exquisitely renegade. She was positioned precisely one inch beyond the sign that demarcated the building's no-smoking zone.

88

"General Dexterity makes robots, right?"

I turned to tell her yes, the company designed industry-leading robot arms for laboratories and—

"You program robot arms, and you bake bread."

"That's right," I said.

"Interesting."

"Is it?"

"Oh, definitely. People here tend to go the other way. They're suspicious of technology."

A jag of excitement skittered through my chest. Was this a hint? "Do you think I'll get a spot?"

She lifted her head in what I thought was going to be the beginning of an affirmative nod, but instead her chin just hung there as she regarded me quietly.

"We'll see."

THE PICKLE PRODUCERS and miscellaneous others all gathered on the main concourse as the Ferry Building's giant clock bonged the hour. Three echoing bongs. The bright-eyed functionary was standing on the catwalk above, and she read off names like a herald calling out the queen's decrees.

I surveyed the crowd. Some faces were plainly tortured with anxiety, on the verge of tears and/or unconsciousness; others appeared placidly pessimistic.

"Gilroy," the functionary called out. The farthest market. She began reading names and products. "Sonja Tarkovsky, tea." There was a little whoop from the very back of the crowd; hundreds of eyes whipped around to find Sonja, some glittering with envy, others with naked malice.

The list went on, Alex and Graham and Jenna, cheese

and coffee and bread—I winced at the bread—and as the crowd shrank, the stakes grew higher. The list was moving north and west, from Gilroy to Los Altos to Colma (a sausage maker slotted there emitted a quiet groan), from Orinda to Moraga to Lake Merritt, closer and closer to the ground on which we stood.

Each vendor accepted made his or her way to a table positioned beside the heirloom bean emporium to receive an orientation packet. The rest of us waited as the markets grew more prestigious and the list grew shorter.

At this point, I maintained no illusions. I would not be chosen.

The functionary came to the end: "For the Ferry Building Farmers Market"—the crowd was silent, levitating an inch off the ground—"we have no selections at this time."

Everyone on the concourse exhaled together, withering disappointment mixed with clean, clear relief. The crowd disintegrated—the force holding it taut was spent—but the functionary wasn't finished. "There's one more," she called out. Most people ignored her; a few turned curious faces toward the catwalk. What could possibly follow the Ferry Building? "For the Marrow Fair," she said, "we have one selection." No one cared. Never heard of it. "Lois Clary, sourdough bread."

It barely registered with any of the others, who were all caught up in celebration or mourning. What was the Marrow Fair? I stared at the functionary. I wasn't sure how to feel; excitement and confusion were duking it out, with horror quietly circling the ring. The functionary caught my gaze and pointed to the table by the beans, where the queen of the underworld waited.

I was so confused I didn't know what questions to ask. Was it real? Was it worth my time? Where was it?

"Hello, baker," the queen of the underworld said. "You weren't selected for one of the main markets, which means I'm free to make an offer. I'm Lily Belasco. I manage the Marrow Fair."

"What . . . is . . . the Marrow Fair?"

She fished something out of her leather jacket. It looked like what was left after you finish a chicken drumstick, but when I accepted it, I realized it wasn't real bone. Instead, it was made from beige plastic, some kind of high-grade polymer, warm and smooth, almost buttery. There was a ring attached to one end, as if to dangle it from a key chain.

"That's a key to my market," Lily Belasco said. "This offer is contingent. But I want you to see the place before you decide."

"Contingent? On what?"

"I'll send you directions. Just come visit. Then decide."

<FROM: BEO>

A LOT OF MAZG WORK in kitchens because (not to sound too haughty, but) we're really very good at it. All the restaurants with Michelin stars, where you can eat salted moss and turnip foam—I guarantee you'll find Mazg working there! I did that in Edinburgh before, at a really excellent restaurant. The owner just found out I was back, and he asked me if I wanted to return. I turned him down. (Nicely.) I've decided I want to open my own restaurant, like in San Francisco, but this time I'm not going to be so cautious about it. I'm not going to be so Mazg!

Lois, I'm telling you before anyone else:

I'm going to have tables.

ALAMEDA

IT WAS SEVEN P.M. when I slunk out of the office with the Clement Street starter in its ceramic crock. Instead of heading home, I walked around the curve of the Embarcadero to the Ferry Building. This time, my destination wasn't the gourmet arcade inside, but the piers beyond. I boarded the boat bound for the skinny island shouldered up against Oakland on the far side of the bay: Alameda.

The trip was shorter than I expected. Soon, we were passing the Port of Oakland and its loading cranes. They looked like the bleached skeletons of prehistoric quadrupeds, Godzilla-scale, with monstrous pulleys in their guts lifting bright containers out of long freighters that dwarfed the ferry.

We bumped up against the dock at Alameda. I disembarked onto a wide parking lot, now mostly empty, and hiked up the road toward the coordinates I'd been given.

I'd never set foot on Alameda before. It had once been home to a sprawling naval base, but that had been decommissioned decades ago, and what remained in its place was a weedy moonscape dotted with military-scale buildings inhabited by small businesses, like hermit crabs in over-large shells. I passed a distillery, a furniture emporium, and a drone manufacturer, each in its own aircraft hangar.

I stopped to check my directions. YES, KEEP WALKING, Lily Belasco had written.

Behind the hangars, there was a huge expanse of abandoned asphalt, cracked and overtaken by vegetation. There were tall grasses and low, tight shrubs with gray-green leaves and bright white blossoms.

I walked across the broken surface, feeling illicit; but there were no fences, no signs telling me to KEEP OUT. It seemed derelict. I passed a hangar-turned-brewery; this was Algebra, whose beers I'd tasted at fancy bars in San Francisco. Their flagship brew was the x^2 Saison.

Out on the airfield, a herd of goats was grazing. They bleated and cried and retreated as I approached, little bells jingling around their necks. It was an unexpected sight: the goats scattered across the vast empty asphalt, gnawing on the patchy grass, and behind them the mirrored quadruped forms of the cranes, snuffling their noses in the holds of the great freighters.

Maybe the cranes would also be improved by bells around their necks.

Among the goats, there were two taller figures. One was an alpaca. It stood in the center of the flock, its gaze tracking me coolly. The other figure was a young man with a rumpled skater look.

I waved, as if signaling a ship, and called out to him. "Hello?"

The man waved lazily, but remained as silent and

baleful as his alpaca accomplice. They both cast very long shadows.

"I'm looking for a market," I shouted. Standing there on the asphalt, it seemed like an absurd statement.

He nodded slowly at this. We were still standing very far apart. The man's aspect and the alpaca's were approximately equivalent: wary, not unfriendly, but fundamentally alien. After a long pause, the man pointed toward the old control tower.

I waved again and walked in that direction.

When I reached the tower, its front door was propped open. I poked my head inside; it appeared long abandoned, scraped clean of furniture and ornament. Spiraling metal steps wound their way upward. Climbing them, I found myself on the tower's bulbous deck with a panoramic view of the airfield and the island and the bay. The window's edge was decorated, through all 360 degrees, with beer bottles, all with Algebra labels. The last of the day's sunlight filtered through them, casting blobs of green light around the room.

The spiraling metal steps returned me to the tower's front door and also continued down into the ground. There was a landing below. I descended and found another door, this one locked tight, blank and gray except for a palm-sized outline stenciled in creamy white paint.

The stencil's shape looked like what was left after you finished a chicken drumstick.

The door offered no knob, no handle, no doorbell, no speakeasy slit. I tried to knock, but the metal hurt my knuckles. I thumped it with my palm. Nothing.

I drew out the buttery plastic bone token I'd received at

the Ferry Building and pressed it against the stencil. From unseen speakers, a synthesized voice bellowed like a buzz saw:

STILL—

TOO—

SKINNY.

And the door opened.

WHILE I WAS IN SAN FRANCISCO with Chaiman, I sometimes had the thought that perhaps the two of us were like the bacteria and the fungus in the starter—a tiny self-sufficient community.

(In that analogy, I am the bacteria and Chaiman is the fungus. Never tell him I said that.)

Chaiman hardly ever comes out of his room anymore. He's working on his album nonstop. He's been talking about it for two years, but something happened after we left San Francisco. He got serious. He follows all the excruciatingly cool music—I don't even understand where he finds it—and he says, "Mazg singing will blow their minds." He's taking the old recordings, cutting them up, transforming them. And, of course, adding a beat. He loves making the beats.

The bacteria stands alone.

PINK LIGHT

I WALKED INTO A SPACE that was long and narrow with the powered-down gloom of a high school at night, a raw concrete concourse with portals all along its edges. Bars of pink light streamed in from those portals and made me think of the prom spilling out of the gym, except here there were many proms, and many gyms, and all were silent. The smooth floor was marked with stripes of paint that had flaked into segments—directions that no one had followed in a long time.

It felt, also, like an empty spaceship, and, as a rule, you do not enter an empty spaceship without first knowing the fate of the crew.

But the floor offered fresher directions, too. Extending away from the door, long strips of yellow tape marked an angling path, and along that path workstations were set up, built from unstained lumber bolted across metal frames supporting kitchen gear and lab equipment. Some workstations had ranges with burners chunky like the grilles of semitrucks. Ventilation hoods whirred softly.

Where—was—the crew?

The workstations had a rough-and-ready look, but this was no shantytown. The floor gleamed; I saw shoe prints over the swirled track of a mop. Power cords snaked across the yellow-tape road, routed securely beneath plastic channels. The arrangement was improvised but not anarchic. There was a power grid. There was a plan.

I stepped off the yellow-tape road to investigate one of the portals and its prom light. Beyond, there was a squarish space about as big as my apartment, the far wall marked *A3* in paint with the same level of flakeage as the stripes on the floor, and both sides of the room were packed with bushy vegetables in trays on tall racks fitted with lights blaring fuchsia. Was that lettuce? Kale? The greens looked black in the weird light. The next portal opened into room A4, which definitely held broccoli. Cauliflower? No, broccoli.

When I turned back to the concourse, it took a moment for my eyes to adjust. I heard the hum of air circulation, the chirp of unseen electronics, and above the hum, below the chirp, I detected murmurs. Voices. The crack of laughter.

I returned to the yellow-tape road, passing more workstations and more pink-light portals on both sides and, in one place, a line of glass-faced industrial refrigerators grumbling and clicking. The road ran straight through them, like a grocery store freezer aisle. The refrigerators were full of tubs and boxes, all with handwritten labels. I shivered.

Ahead, the road bent sharply around a line of enormous planter boxes supporting bushy, dark-leafed trees, their branches heavy with lemons. Above them, the ceiling broke open and admitted a cylinder of hazy sunlight through a smudgy grid of glass.

On the other side of the pop-up lemon grove, I found the

crew—dozens strong, all sitting together at a superlong picnic table, talking and eating. Tattoos flashed on wrists and forearms as they passed dishes and poked forks. Men and women, mostly young, but a few with gray hair or bald heads.

Near the middle of the table, a figure rose. It was the queen of the underworld in her slouchy black leather jacket: Lily Belasco.

"Baker!" she called.

A few heads swiveled, and those few regarded me amiably. Belasco beckoned, and I went to her, holding my bone-key token in front of me as I approached, as if it were an amulet of protection. "You invited me here," I said. A reminder, and maybe also an accusation.

Belasco wiggled her hands and the people sitting across from her scooched apart dutifully. I wedged myself between them—a man and a woman. The man, who was broad-bellied and round-cheeked, began building a plate. The woman, who was as tiny as an elf, reached for an unlabeled growler and filled a jam jar with dark beer.

"This is Lois," Belasco said to everyone within earshot, "a very talented baker." This was followed by silence. I got the sense maybe everyone within earshot was a very talented baker. Belasco continued: "She also programs robots." That earned a raised eyebrow from the elf girl and a few murmurs of interest farther down. "Lois, this is Horace"—the round-cheeked man—"who managed the bookstore at the Ferry Building before joining us as our . . . What are you, Horace, the archivist?"

"Librarian," Horace said neatly.

"And this is Orli"—the elf—"who sells cheese."

I looked down at the plate Horace had built for me: brown rice with green onions and sesame seeds, dark glistening greens, a curl of what appeared . . . to be . . . octopus. I'd never eaten octopus. I looked up at Lily Belasco. "What is this place?"

She waved the question away. "First, eat. Gracie was just showing us her new acquisition." She turned to the woman next to her, wide-framed with dark freckles, who cupped a jar on the table in front of her.

"Chernobyl honey," Gracie said.

"Surely not," Belasco scoffed.

Gracie nodded firmly. "It's gone back to nature," she explained, "and the bees, they filter out the radioactivity. Most. Enough." She unscrewed the jar, offered a taste. Belasco dipped her spoon and lifted it, trailing a strand that seemed to glow faintly. Put it between her lips, let it sit. Her eyes glittered. "Try it," she said to all of us seated around her. "Try it, try it."

The elf—Orli—dipped her spoon. Horace dipped his, too, and from him the Chernobyl honey earned a rumble of appreciation that was conducted by the bench into the soft flesh of my thighs.

Gracie tipped the jar toward me. "Try some, baker." The gesture was solicitous, but her eyes glinted challenge.

In every legend of the underworld, there is the same warning: Don't eat the food. Not before you know what's happening and/or what bargain you're accepting.

Along the length of the table, wide dishes bobbed up and down, orbiting on currents of camaraderie. I saw faces smiling and serious, all lit by the hazy light from above, but haloed with pink from the portals on both sides. Across the table, Lily Belasco watched me with dark eyes. I had come this far.

I dipped my spoon.

I N SAN FRANCISCO, there was an older woman, a Russian, the sister of Shehrieh's landlord in Brussels from long ago, back before either Chaiman or I was born. (I'm laughing here, because this is how every Mazg story starts: "My old landlord." The Mazg are inveterate renters.) Anyway, this Russian owns many buildings on Clement Street. She offered us an apartment, but the kitchen had no oven, just a hot plate, and when we asked for a different one, she said, You're going to get me in trouble! But she couldn't refuse, because many years ago, Shehrieh did something very kind for her sister.

This is such a Mazg story, it's sort of embarrassing.

Anyway, Chaiman and I got an apartment with an oven. It wasn't very big, but I felt comfortable there, and that's where the phone rang when you called me all those times.

THE FAUSTOFEN

THE MARROW FAIR is a new kind of market," Lily Belasco explained. Picnic dinner was over and everyone who had tasted the Chernobyl honey was still alive. I was following her away from the lemon grove, back up the yellow-tape road, the way I'd come. "It's an experiment, a place for new ideas. New tools. New food."

"What is this *place*, though?" I asked.

"Oh. Back when the base was operational, this was a munitions depot. Don't you love it? Long and skinny, like a mirror-image Ferry Building."

Like an *underworld* Ferry Building. Yes, I could see why this space appealed to Lily Belasco. As above, so below!

"They kept missiles down here," she continued. "Lifted them up through there"—she pointed back toward the skylight—"into planes, I guess? Don't worry. The floor isn't radioactive anymore."

There was a lot of weird light for a place that wasn't radioactive . . .

"Those are grow rooms. All pink LEDs! Apparently, plants

absorb that portion of the spectrum more efficiently. Ask Kenyatta, he'll tell you more."

Belasco pointed out workstations as we passed them: "That's the coffee bar. Naz Kalil runs it—he was Greenlight Coffee's first barista. Over there they make a new kind of smoothie. Look closely before you try one. Around that corner—cricket cookies. I can smell them. Mmm."

We arrived at a place close to the door where I'd entered, far from the light of the lemon grove. There was a workstation here, shadowed and bare. "Here we are. This is where I want you and your robot."

There had been a misunderstanding. "I don't have a robot. I just work on them."

Belasco groped the depot's wall to find a switch that brought cold fluorescent tubes sparking to life above the workstation. It was outfitted with the same basic accoutrements as the rest—a countertop, some wire shelves, an industrial sink—and it boasted, in addition, a ping-pong table with no net, one folding chair (currently folded), and, finally, an elephantine bread oven, gray and stoic, the size of a small car.

Belasco gave me a frank look. "A market in the Bay Area needs, at minimum, three things. It needs fancy coffee, weird honey, and sourdough bread. Naz has been here from the start and he roasts his beans with lasers. Gracie gets me my honey. You might be my baker. But like I said, this is a place for new tools." She smiled. "I want robot bread."

"I don't. Have. A robot."

She looked at me innocently. "Get one."

"Why can't I just bake bread normally?"

"Go to Colma if you want to do that. I need you to do something different here. The new ideas, they're not always . . . Have you seen cricket flour? It looks like flour. Once you explain it, people get interested, but as we approach our opening, I am mindful of the need for a bit more pizzazz. You, baker, could provide this pizzazz."

I had never before been invited to provide the pizzazz.

"Get a robot and this spot is yours. You'll have the exclusive sourdough franchise. The market runs previews Wednesday mornings. Look, you're right by the door! You'll sell out. Get a robot."

MY DISGRUNTLEMENT DISSOLVED on contact with the problem, the way it had hundreds of times at Crowley and General Dexterity. Maybe that was my great weakness: if a task was even mildly challenging, any sense of injustice drained away and I simply worked quietly until I was done.

I guess I learned that in school.

The elephantine bread oven's manufacturer was etched on the thin lip of metal above the baking bays; it was a FAUSTOFEN, from MUNICH. I looked it up on Global Gluten— the depot had very fast wireless internet, network name: CRUCIFEROUS—and discovered that the oven was considered a boring but reliable workhorse of industrial bakeries.

A Faustofen definitely did not provide pizzazz.

It took me a bit of poking around to find an open pantry stocked with staples, including flour and salt, the latter Diamond Crystal, which made me feel for a moment like I was somewhat in the loop. I mixed the flour with water and fed the Clement Street starter, watched it bubble and fizz. It was late, nearly midnight, but I was wide-awake, buoyed by curiosity. We would see about pizzazz. I mixed some dough and set it to rest.

I stood and faced the Faustofen. The controls were all in German, but how difficult could they be? Very difficult, it turned out. It took me ten minutes to deduce the combination that commanded ignition. When I did, the deep *whoomph* of the burners inside sent me leaping backward.

As I turned the dough, I paid special attention to what my joints were doing. I imagined myself a General Dexterity robot arm. I made low, rumbling robot-arm noises.

A smell wafted over from farther up the concourse, fishy and marine. I heard the clink of glass. I watched a sheet of steam rise in the distance. I saw a woman in a short lab coat, stunningly beautiful, dark-skinned with darker slashes under her eyes, wandering slowly up the yellow-tape road carrying a bright blue mug, her lips moving slightly, twitching at moments into a smile. Then, suddenly, she spun in place and sprinted back to wherever she'd been working.

I knew that feeling.

While I waited for the dough to rise, I wandered back to the lemon grove and the coffee bar. The barista, Naz, alternated his attention between a rig upon which a laser tracked slowly across a scattered bed of coffee beans—their roasty smell rising—and a laptop that showed a long playlist.

"Any requests?" he asked.

It was only then that I became aware of the depot's soundtrack: currently an ambient swell so deep it could have been the far-off foghorns that guarded the Golden Gate.

Was it the far-off foghorns?

"She calls herself Microclimate," Naz explained. "She

samples the foghorns up close, then she plays with the sound, turns it into drums, voices, everything."

So Naz chose the Marrow Fair's music.

"The acoustics in here," he began, and then words failed him, and he just shook his head in awe.

I sat with my cappuccino in the folding chair alongside the ping-pong table. The acoustics of the concourse carried not only Naz's playlist but also scraps of sound from other workstations. I heard low beeps, sharp scrapes, muttered conferences, and the occasional laugh. The depot was wreathed in gentle effort. It percolated.

My dough had risen, so I formed a loaf. Technically, I should have let it sit, but I was impatient. I slung it into the Faustofen's top baking bay and commanded the stoic monolith to bake.

The Faustofen had, in addition to its temperature dial, a humidity control, and I'd never controlled an oven's humidity before. I made my best guess and resolved to check Global Gluten later. Then, through cloudy glass, I watched the solitary loaf bake. It felt transgressive; a process previously private, protected by walls three bricks thick, now starkly visible.

Naz must have switched albums, because the foghorn faded to nothing and was replaced by electronic drums—slow taps blurred by the width and breadth of the concourse into massive echoing thuds. I imagined the loading cranes at the Port of Oakland lifting their legs to plod across the airfield above.

Inside the Faustofen, the loaf inflated.

The crust darkened. Cracks formed.

A face emerged, wearing just the faintest smile.

I looked around. I liked this spot, right next to the door. I liked the folding chair. I liked the ping-pong table. I liked the pink light and the cool soundtrack and the wandering geniuses.

It couldn't be that difficult to acquire a robot arm.

<FROM: BEO>

So, you asked about the starter.

The Mazg have many stories explaining how it came to us, and they all contradict each other. Every family maintains their own starter, always in a ceramic crock like the one I gave you. Sometimes the crocks are very old. That one was pretty new. I bought it in Daly City.

Here in Edinburgh, in the little Mazg neighborhood, when I go walking in the morning, through all the second-story windows I can hear the starters singing.

REFURB

I TOLD PETER I wanted to borrow a robot arm so I could teach it to bake bread.

"I don't eat bread," he reminded me.

That was well established.

"I didn't think the arms could do kitchen stuff," Peter said.

"They can't. Not yet. I can figure it out."

He pressed his lips together and I saw the muscles of his jaw working. This was Peter's being-a-manager face. It meant he was figuring out how to help you. "There's never enough arms, and Task allocates them. But if you really think you can do it . . . Huh. That would be a big deal, right? It would be. We could pitch it to Andrei."

For all his reality-bending intensity, our CEO was accessible and approachable. He ate his lunch in the cafeteria with the rest of us, sitting with a different group every day. You could tell where he was without looking because Andrei's table always laughed a little too loud.

Peter and I went to lunch early. We migrated between the stations of the cafeteria slowly, smoothie to salad to waffle maker, circling vulture-like, waiting for Andrei to appear.

Peter looked very suspicious circling with just a single green Tetra Pak.

When Andrei appeared, Peter hooted an alert, and I tracked the CEO out the tail of my eye. It took him a long time to fill his tray—every step interrupted by a greeting, an admonition, a whispered report. I had never watched him this closely. Passing through the cafeteria, he left a wake of keyed-up expressions—smiles and grimaces. He was a walking amphetamine. Peter and I loitered together at the paella station. My pulse accelerated.

Finally, Andrei selected a seat at a half-empty table.

"Go, go, go!" Peter commanded. We sprinted across the cafeteria, Peter angling neatly between the Dextrous, me smashing into them, to bring our butts—his sliding, mine crashing—into the table's last available chairs. Two cold-eyed wraiths had been vectoring for the same spots. I glared at them and sounded a warning hiss.

"Peter!" Andrei boomed. "And Lois!" He looked around the table. "Do you all know Peter and Lois? Peter runs Control, and Lois works on Proprioception. Very cool stuff."

Andrei knew everyone's name and role. Everyone's. It was said he used flash cards.

Peter and I had planned to begin with three to five minutes of small talk before easing into our overture, but looking at the group of Dextrous we had joined, I understood suddenly that everyone at the table had exactly the same plan. We were not the only birds of prey in this cafeteria.

"*The eggs!*" I blurted.

Andrei raised an eyebrow.

"I want to solve the egg problem," I said. "I mean. Cooking. Specifically, baking."

Andrei lifted a curl of fennel from the top of his salad and popped it into his mouth, where he chewed it thoughtfully.

Peter daintily removed the seal from his Tetra Pak.

The other Dextrous glowered.

"We've been working on that for a long time," Andrei said.

"Right. But I know the Control codebase, and I know the task."

"An integrated approach," Peter interjected.

I nodded. We had practiced. "Task and Control together."

Peter couldn't help himself. "But if it works, Control gets the credit."

We had the rest of the argument ready to go—an appeal to the skunkworks spirit, a preapproved interjection from Peter praising my most recent bug fix—but none of it was needed. Andrei nodded, picked up his phone, and tapped a short message.

"Okay. You can have a refurbished arm. Lois, this is your job now. Peter, you'll oversee?"

Peter slurped affirmatively.

"Great. Make it work."

I told him thank you, and that I was going to sit somewhere else to actually eat my lunch. Andrei laughed (followed by everyone else at the table, too loudly) and waved me away.

Later, I crossed Townsend to meet my new robot at the Task Acquisition Center. I walked through the rows of arms, watched them lift boxes and knock over glass bottles. I walked all the way to the back of the building, to a work area set up against the far wall, where several arms stood slack, all of them marked with wide red stickers that said REFURB.

A woman was sitting at a small desk there in the shadows: Deborah Palmer-Grill, queen of the training floor.

DPG narrowed her eyes. "So I hear you're going to solve the egg problem."

I nodded slowly.

"We've broken a lot of eggs in here."

"I'm going to try something different."

"More eggs than you can imagine. Garbage bins full of shells. Full of them!"

"I'm going to bring you a loaf of bread," I said with more confidence than I actually possessed. "It's going to be perfect, and it's going to be baked by this . . . fellow . . . right here." I patted the closest arm.

"Not that one," DPG said. "That one's new. The one on the end—that's a Vitruvian 3 from a year ago. Fill out this form. They used that one at the CDC, so if I were you, I'd wipe it down extra good."

THE ARM ARRIVED on the airfield borne on a pallet, mummified in plastic wrap, delivered by a courier waiting confusedly on the asphalt whose relief showed clearly when we appeared from inside the control tower. Lily Belasco and I extracted the Vitruvian, released the brakes on its wheeled base, and brought it slowly down the vehicle ramp into the depot, Belasco cackling the whole way.

IS IT STRANGE that a sourdough starter sings?

It didn't seem strange when I was a child. I'm now twenty-three years old (how old are you?), and yes, I understand that most starters don't behave this way. But I still don't think the singing is the most remarkable thing about it. (I'm not being evasive—this is the truth.) Every time I feed my family's starter, I feel a sense of awe, because from your starter to mine to my mother's and her father's, it's all the *same stuff,* and it goes back a very long way. Immortality is stranger than singing, if you ask me.

Anyway, Leopold says it's just a weird thing with the CO_2 bubbles.

In other news, I have officially received permission from Chaiman to share one of his new tracks. It's attached.

CATHEDRALS

THE MARROW FAIR'S ORIENTATION wasn't as involved as I'd expected, given that I was being granted space in a repurposed munitions depot slightly below sea level. Lily Belasco showed me the bathrooms, told me there were emergency exits in most but not all directions, then pressed a flashlight into my palm. She explained that the depot connected to other bygone facilities that were not fully mapped.

"But really," she said, "nothing's radioactive anymore."

I resolved to orient myself. The concourse was the spine of the Marrow Fair, and the lemon grove, with the skylight above, its central chakra. Beyond that, portals opened not into pink light but darkness, and long corridors. Exploring them, I discovered:

- A mushroom grotto where dense clusters of broad-brimmed fungi protruded from transparent plastic sacks bulging with dark dirt.
- The cricket farm! I did not see the bugs, but I heard them, chittering enormously in the darkness. I turned and retreated.

- A single lemon, forlorn and desiccated.
- A ladder that rose to a hatch. When I poked my head through, I found myself nearly nose to nose with one of the goats grazing on the airfield. It regarded me with flat skepticism. (Goats only ever give side-eye.)
- An enormous vehicle ramp, wide enough for whatever kind of truck carries (nuclear?) missiles. I hiked its gentle rise to find myself at the back of the Algebra hangar with its gleaming vats. Brewers rolled kegs on dollies and bantered about the recent performance of the Golden State Warriors. I wandered out through the brewery onto the airfield and saw the goats again in the distance.

I went back down and followed the concourse to its terminus, a blank concrete wall with another gray door marked with a stencil and unlocked by the bone key: *STILL—TOO—SKINNY*. This door opened onto the glittering water and the night sky and a tiny concrete pier at which a wide-bellied boat waited with a few passengers, familiar from inside, already seated in her stern. I returned to San Francisco on that slow, easygoing craft, and learned from its pilot that he operated a daily ferry service for the Marrow Fair. He gave me a slip of paper on which his schedule was printed alongside his name, Carl, as well as the name of his boat, the *Omebushi*.

His schedule started at six a.m. "Is that the earliest?" I asked.

"You need me to go earlier?"

I told him I might.

He nodded gravely. "Just means more hours for me and the *'Bushi*. I'll tell Belasco."

LATER, I FOUND MY ROUND-CHEEKED NEIGHBOR from the picnic table. His full name was Horace Portacio and he was the Marrow Fair's librarian. He also compiled the weekly e-newsletter.

In a prime spot just across the yellow-tape road from the lemon trees, he tended his own dark grove of bookshelves, and beside them a field of legal boxes, which held thousands of menus from restaurants famous and obscure. Whenever I passed Horace's collection, there was someone flipping through the menus with the furious intensity of a DJ digging in the crates.

When I introduced myself again and explained I'd officially joined the market, Horace raised a finger—*Just a moment!*—then disappeared into his shelves. He emerged again with a teetering armload of books. It seemed impossible that he had gathered them so quickly. Did he have thematic stacks presorted, awaiting the right recipient? He sat to enumerate the volumes.

"Here we have a reproduction of a pamphlet printed by the bakers guild in London, around, let's see, 1600, very nice. And *A History of Food*, it's quite contemporary"—he said that with palpable regret—"but there's a good bit on baking. And here, oh yes, these"—he plopped a folder onto the table—"are Edward Brown's notes toward *The Tassajara Bread Book*. Lovely handwriting, don't you think? Keep those pages together. And of course you must read Ibn Butlan. Here is his classic *Tacuinum Sanitatis*, an edition printed around 1500. There's a section where he strongly recommends whole wheat, and I, for one, am inclined to obey. And of course . . ." He flipped through *Tacuinum Sanitatis*, searching for a page, and when he found it, he spun the book around to show me. "That," Horace said, "is the first identifiable published illustration of a carrot." He was beaming.

The book looked very old. I didn't want to take it.

"Oh, you must, you must!" he said. "It is an absolutely foundational document."

I squinted at the text below the illustration. "I can't read Latin."

Horace sobered. "All right. I'll keep this one. But take the rest."

THE NEXT DAY, I rode the *Omebushi* from San Francisco to Alameda, used my bone-key token to enter through the bay door, loaded the master development branch of ArmOS into my refurbished Vitruvian 3, and spent the next six hours teaching it to stir.

With my fingers on its elbows, I led it through the motion. This was Task Segmentation. Whenever I paused and said, "Like that," the Vitruvian emitted a whispering beep of acknowledgment, recording not only the motion but also its understanding of the context—what it saw through its cameras (visible and thermal) and felt through its pressure sensors. After finishing the sequence, I stepped back and spoke again. "Now you try."

And so it came to pass that a late-model Vitruvian, loaded with the master development branch of ArmOS, reenacted all the horrors of my first attempts at baking.

Except this arm was five feet long, with strength commensurate, and every error was multiplied. It sent the bowl clanging across the concrete, leaving a powdery trail of unmixed flour.

I did, in time, teach it to stir, and so we progressed, briefly, to kneading and shaping, but then it was launching disks of dough through the air like gooey artillery. The arm was strong; they went a long way. One of the disks missed the coffee bar by inches. One of them, I never found.

For now, we would stick to stirring.

THE FLUX OF PREVIEW CUSTOMERS in the Marrow Fair when the doors opened the following Wednesday morning was immense. Had these people all been waiting out on the airfield, jostling with the goats? Between eight and nine a.m., the depot transformed from a spaceship into . . . a farmers market on a spaceship. The customers looked, for the most part, very rich. I saw the toothsome plaids of tech wealth, and I saw the supple leather handbags of something older.

The customers came gliding through the control tower door, none in any rush, some walking alone, others in pairs or small groups whispering among themselves. I hadn't yet taught the Vitruvian to do anything of value, so my workstation stood quiet and dark while they passed.

Horace approached me. "Shall we wander?" he asked. "It's always interesting to see what everyone is offering."

There was Gracie with her Chernobyl honey; the cave-dwelling mushroom monger; a man and a woman decanting smoothies that appeared to have . . . *things* swimming inside them. Orli, the elf, presided over a table piled with cheeses, some ghostly pale, some brown like leather, and some veined not only with blue but also bright green and hot pink. The larger wheels she had carved into pieces at irregular angles, so the resulting hunks looked like soft, fat jewels.

There was a workstation selling algorithmically optimized bagels, their outsides perfectly smooth like computer renderings. A printed banner said NEWBAGEL; it was surprisingly well designed.

There was a man selling barramundi that lived their whole lives in watery tubes extending deep into the depot's corridors. Next to him, another man cleaned those fish and fried them into tacos on the spot, filling tortillas made from cricket flour and topping them with slaw made from cabbage grown in the pink-light rooms. Horace and I requested two tacos each and agreed that the collaboration was impeccable.

We came to the cricket bakery and Horace greeted its proprietor. "Anita! This is Lois, a baker of great skill. She employs a robot." To me, Horace said, "You must try one of Anita's cookies." It was light brown, threaded with darker grains. "There are cave paintings in Spain, thirty thousand years old, that depict the collection and consumption of insects." He popped a cookie into his mouth.

When we moved on, I asked him, "So who are these customers? If one of them says, 'Sure, Anita, I'll take a dozen boxes of bug cookies . . .'?"

Horace leaned closer, clearly delighted to be conspiring. "I believe we have here representatives of many of the greatest restaurants in the world—from San Francisco, New York, London, and Tokyo. Who better to assess the market's progress? They bring their findings to their diners. Perhaps they report back to Mr. Marrow, as well."

We approached the lemon grove. Just ahead, a young woman held court before several of the customers. She was the one I'd seen the first night, walking the quiet concourse carrying a mug of coffee and an inward look.

"—a nutritionally complete food product," she was saying. The stitching on her lab coat named her DR. JAINA MITRA.

The woman was passing around a platter stacked with blocks of apparently edible matter. Each was wrapped in silvery-green paper, but the matter itself was as white as a grub. The blocks resembled ghostly Rice Krispies Treats.

The customers moved along, one whispering to another. Jaina Mitra's gaze followed them. She chewed her lip a little.

"Hello, Dr. Mitra," Horace said. "This is Lois. She has a robot."

Jaina Mitra said hello, her eyes still following the customers, and absently offered the platter to us.

I lifted a slab and gave it an exploratory sniff. It smelled like dirt. Not in a bad way. "You said it's nutritionally complete. Is this anything like Slurry?"

Jaina Mitra's gaze snapped around. "No," she said, her face taut. "This is Lembas. It's much better. Have you tried Slurry?"

When I told her that I had, in fact, subsisted on it, she looked surprised. "Lembas is a very different concept. I'll explain, but please, taste it first."

I took a bite, expecting the slippery, chemical tang that I knew from Slurry. Instead, the taste was warm and definite. The closest comparison was an immense tater tot, but it went beyond tot; in this substance, the balance of sponge to crisp was perfected.

I ate the whole piece.

Jaina Mitra smiled. "You like it?"

It tasted great, and the initial texture was top-notch, but

once inside my mouth it seemed to surrender to my saliva too easily. I could feel it adhering to my molars.

"Itsh good," I said, "but"—swallowing—"itsh a bit shticky."

"Mmf," Horace mumbled in agreement. He was struggling to unstick his jaws.

"That's the new enzymes," Jaina Mitra said darkly. "I should make a note." She scrambled back to her workstation, typed something into her laptop, then turned back.

"Whatsh it shupposed—" I started. "Wait." I squeegeed my teeth with my tongue. "What's it supposed to taste like?"

Jaina Mitra's gaze sharpened. "Nothing. It's not intended to be a simulation. I think food should taste like what it is, don't you? And what this *is*, is a super-nutritious cellulosic suspension manufactured in situ by a community of microbes."

Jaina Mitra was, I decided, very impressive.

"It's got all the vitamins, minerals, and macronutrients you need," she said, "all in the right ratios. Plenty of protein. Tons of fiber. *Tons.*"

Horace had regained his powers of speech. "Dr. Mitra, you are the heir to Pasteur!" he exclaimed. "Mistress of microbes. I believe Bruno Latour would be tickled by this. I have a book of his you should read . . ."

Jaina Mitra turned to the machine that stood behind her, occupying most of the workstation: an enormous steel cylinder with a bright, swirly logo on its breast, from which burst a tangle of pipes and cables. One large pipe connected the cylinder to a wide beige box with the plain *Who, me?* look that all biotech gear seemed to share.

"This is my bioreactor," she said, accents of pride evident on both *my* and *bioreactor.* She looked at me, ready to make a point. "As you might know, Slurry is assembled from various organic precursors. Basically thrown together in a blender." Her voice made it clear she did not respect mere blending. "My Lembas cakes are manufactured whole by living microorganisms."

I pointed to the shiny cylinder. "Right there in that tank?"

"Bioreactor. Yes. I grow the cultures here, and they assemble the cakes here."

She opened one of her huge cabinets, which was populated by racks that looked like shallow muffin trays. In each one, a Lembas cake was blooming: the light, airy structure rising like scaffolding. Around their edges, they glistened wetly.

"The form recalls a Breton cake," Horace mused. "It almost has the finesse of a kouign-amann."

"I think of them as microbial cathedrals," Jaina Mitra said.

I wondered if that comparison made her the architect or the deity.

"Why not just leave it liquid like Slurry?" I asked.

Jaina Mitra ticked off the reasons: "Mouthfeel. Dental health. Market research indicates people associate liquid superfood with pessimistic science fiction." That was a good point. "And, I should clarify, I don't want people to eat Lembas all day, every day," she said. "It's your quick lunch. It's what you eat in the car. It solves food security, because once I get the microbial community stabilized, we'll be able to produce it literally *anywhere*. Trust me, I have no desire to replace all of this." She lifted her hands to encompass the Marrow Fair. "It's fast food I want to replace, and all the other terrible stuff people eat when they get impatient."

"Starbucks breakfast sandwiches," I said ruefully.

"*Curse* those breakfast sandwiches," Horace muttered.

Jaina Mitra offered the platter again. "Another one?"

I ran my tongue around my teeth, found bits of cathedral still stuck there. "I'm fine for now."

"Come back for the next batch," she said. "I'm going to get those enzymes dialed in. It's almost ready. Almost, almost, *almost* ready."

<FROM: BEO>

RIGHT NOW, I'M MAKING SPICY SOUP, the kind you like. Chaiman brought his laptop into the kitchen (Shehrieh told him he was being a weird hermit) and he's hunched over the table, composing. I can hear the *oonce-oonce* in his headphones. As for my mother, she's rolling noodles on the countertop, humming while she does it.

It always begins with the humming. Chaiman and I joke about this. It sneaks up on her. In another minute, she'll be singing with her full voice. She can't help herself. Right now, she's humming her favorite song, which is about leaving places behind, and how it's sad but also happy.

It's very Mazg.

Lois, the picture you sent—the robot with the mixing bowl—it inspired me. I think I've gotten complacent with my cooking. I need to experiment more! This morning I separated a bit of my starter and mixed some Fresno chili into its food.

It died instantly.

But I'm not giving up! If you want to experiment, too, we

could compare notes. For one thing, I recommend feeding your starter better flour. It's hard to get good flour in the U.S., but it makes a big difference.

My stockpile of Fresno chilies is dwindling, by the way.

THIS NEW DARKNESS

THE NEXT WEDNESDAY, I was ready. When the preview customers streamed in, their eyes snapped onto the Vitruvian, and they murmured appreciative sounds to one another. Not many stopped; there were stranger delights than sourdough bread waiting within. But this is what they wanted to see. This is where they wanted to be.

I understood Belasco's objective now. I was a mascot. I was the pizzazz.

I saw faces I vaguely recognized from the world of General Dexterity. A young tech CEO; several well-known investors; a programmer with a wine blog.

Two men stopped to assess the Vitruvian. It was, in fact, a pair of the cold-eyed wraiths I worked with at General Dexterity. I knew them by their sneakers.

"Oh, *sweet*," hooted one. "Didn't expect to see a V3 here."

"Look at that beast," said the other.

"It's so clunky, dude! The old motors were super slow."

"Actually," I said—oh, it felt good—"the Vitruvian 3's motors are exactly the same as the V4's. They're all PKD 2891s. It's just that the V4's chassis is lighter."

The wraiths noticed me for the first time. "Wait," said the first. "I know you, right? You're . . . one of our marketing people?"

My face burned hot, but through force of will, I cooled my gaze to absolute zero kelvin. "Actually." Yes. It felt very good. "I work on Control."

The wraiths pulled knives from their waistbands and committed ritual suicide.

Actually, they backed slowly away, and I never saw them again.

A pear-shaped, plaid-shirted customer stopped to admire first the Vitruvian and then the loaves with their merry faces. "What's, uh, going on with these, exactly?" he asked.

I explained to the pear-shaped man in plaid that I was offering sourdough bread made from a starter strange and potent that had come into my possession unexpectedly. I explained that I found the bread delicious and also mood-stabilizing. I explained that the faces were a trade secret.

Oh, and a robot mixed the dough.

He lifted a loaf, tapped it on its back with his finger, listened to the sound, and for a moment, his expression matched the loaf's. He dug for his wallet. I was officially in business.

By nine a.m., the loaves were gone. I had to turn away a customer, and in her eyes I saw a glint of covetousness. She would be back next Wednesday, I understood suddenly. She would be here earlier.

I darkened my workstation and walked, buzzed on commerce. Did I need another Faustofen? How much bread could one morning market absorb? Could this grow into a real business, a real bakery? Would I have my nineteen million dollars?

Up and down the concourse, the Marrow Fair had been sucked dry. Orli's table was bare, her gemlike cheeses all claimed for various hoards. The pink-light farmers had retreated into their grow rooms to tend their crops. The fishmonger's cooler was empty, and only crumbs remained at the bug bakery. Even Naz's stock was depleted. He'd run out of milk and could offer only unadulterated espresso.

The only person with anything left was Jaina Mitra. She stood beside the yellow-tape road with her platter of Lembas cakes, smiling at the last straggling customers as they skirted her lab on their way toward the exit. Her cathedrals were fascinating . . . but not yet appealing.

After that, my days were cleaved in two.

I rose earlier than ever before and experienced a portion of the morning that was new to me. I heard the chirping of unfamiliar bird species—negotiations that had, until now, been concluded long before I woke. The bus didn't run that early, so I bought a used bicycle, paying $50 cash to a woman outside Velo Rouge Cafe, and pedaled my new route: cutting south from Cabrillo Street to ride through Golden Gate Park on my way to the Wiggle, which would take me to Market Street and, at its terminus, the Ferry Building, locked tight.

In this new darkness, I pushed my bicycle to the pier where the *Omebushi* waited. Carl offered me coffee from a family-size thermos. It was just the two of us crossing the bay, and when the fat little boat puttered below the bulk of the Bay Bridge, I felt like we were astronauts in transit across the back side of the moon.

In this new darkness, the Marrow Fair welcomed me. The computerized *STILL—TOO—SKINNY* became rote and comforting. Naz's morning playlist echoed through the concourse, lazy and hopeful. Even in those hours, the depot was never empty. There was always someone—multiple someones—who had spent the night working. Aromas wafted. Timers beeped. Crickets chirped.

In this new darkness, my team greeted me. The Faustofen woke with the *whoomph* of burners. The Vitruvian snapped to life with a friendly chime and leapt instantly to work, arranging its tools in a neat line. The forming of the loaves still eluded it, but I'd taught it to reach the sink and wash the mixing bowls. That was something.

In this new darkness, the Clement Street starter greeted me like a puppy, yapping and leaping, excited to be alive.

In this new darkness, a catalog of phenomena:

- Ripples across its surface like laughter
- Bursts of luminescence, like the signal flare from before, but brighter, shifting from green to pink
- A tiny pseudopod rising slowly like a periscope, wobbling back and forth, then retracting into the crock
- Songs, various: wider-ranging, not just imitations of Chaiman's CD, but new sounds it was picking up in the depot, including a soft but unmistakable foghorn
- Scents, various: still banana, always, along with smoky smells, like far-off fires, and occasionally the scent of gasoline

In this new darkness, I baked as fast as I could: taking dough from the Vitruvian, forming loaves, slamming them into the Faustofen.

Then, while the Vitruvian stirred another batch of dough and the Clement Street starter performed its last labors in the oven, I cracked my laptop and did the work of the Dextrous, responding to emails, reviewing code. I was preternaturally productive in those hours. At first I theorized it was something about the rhythm of baking, the quick bursts of attention alternating with mandatory pauses, but then I decided it was probably something simpler: I was happy.

Most days, I gathered my loaves and rode the *Omebushi* back to San Francisco, still in darkness, to deliver them to Chef Kate.

On Wednesdays, I kept baking while the market opened for its preview hour. I called out, "Arm, change task. Say hello!" and the customers waved back. Loaves came out of the Faustofen and disappeared in moments. Pizzazz! As soon as I sold out, I patted the Vitruvian on the shoulder, powered it down, covered the starter in its crock, made for the *Omebushi*, and watched the sun rise over the Oakland hills from the middle of the bay.

My work complete, I went to work.

At lunchtime, I sat with the Slurry contingent in the General Dexterity cafeteria, but it had been weeks since I consumed any of the nutritive gel myself. I ate my own product: sourdough bread slathered with butter or soft avocado, consumed with gusto while Peter looked on ruefully.

AT BEO'S URGING, I upgraded my flour. The cheap stuff had served me well, but this new phase called for a finer grain. There was a mill just fifty miles away, in a farm town west of Davis, that sold flour ground from wheat grown nearby. It cost more than twice as much as King Arthur flour, so I started small, with just a little bag, a test run.

The Clement Street starter loved it. It groaned and luxuriated. It belched ecstatically.

There was more to upgrade. I went to a shop in downtown Oakland that sold salt of every kind and color, black and pink and blue. Each variety sat shimmering in a glass canister, priced by the ounce, with a handwritten card recounting its biography: here, salt from the beaches of Gujarat; there, salt from the pans of Brittany; behold, salt from the suburbs of Portland.

I backed slowly out the door. I would stick with Diamond Crystal.

At the Marrow Fair, I sought out Gracie, the woman with the Chernobyl honey, and the starter's next feeding included a thin drizzle of the stuff. The morning after that, it glowed brighter than ever before, and when the loaves emerged, their expressions looked slightly wonky. I took a picture and shared my findings with Beoreg.

I WAS GETTING HEALTHY.

My arms were stronger, from working the dough. My legs were thicker, from riding my bicycle. My butt showed a heretofore unimagined definition. Even with all the bread I was eating—and it was not a small amount—I lost ten pounds. I felt lean and purposeful. Scoping myself out in my stand-up mirror, I turned and gently twerked.

In the evening—it was possibly more accurate to call it late afternoon—when I fell into my bed, I was truly tired; not merely the brain-spent *Well, I guess I'll give up now* tiredness of a day at the robot factory, but something deeper, actually muscular.

Weeks passed in a haze of happy exhaustion.

In this new darkness, once every two weeks, I found waiting on the ping-pong table an envelope, and inside a check issued by the Patelco Credit Union under the authority of an ALAMEDA TEST MARKET, LLC, bearing the angular signature of *Lily Belasco*. My earnings, minus the market's percentage. The amount was not staggering—barely a tenth of my General Dexterity paycheck for the same amount of time—but this money felt more truly mine, somehow.

In this new darkness, I stood behind the ping-pong table, considered the Clement Street starter in its crock and my partner the brawny Vitruvian. The hardy Faustofen, too. I looked out across the depot, awash in pink light, the tang of tube-fish rising, and realized it was the hidden root of something interesting and maybe important, and I, improbably, was part of it.

WE'RE MOVING AGAIN! Shehrieh decided suddenly, and when you're Mazg, you don't question this feeling. Our destination is Berlin. It's actually going to be perfect. Even though Berlin is a bigger city than Edinburgh, the Mazg community there is smaller. I'm thinking strategically, you see.

I just finished packing our kitchen things into boxes. I wish we could take the oven. It's a good one—a very old and beautiful English model. I told our landlord she could sell it on the internet. Someone in California would buy it in a second, then pay just as much again to ship it across the world.

I still haven't told anyone else about my restaurant. This is good practice, to say it, or write it. I'm nervous. Shehrieh will be worried because we're supposed to be "the second-story people." Leopold will be worried just because he worries. But I want those tables! I want a sign, written in German *and* in Mazg. I want a front door with a little bell that rings when people step inside.

I'm starting my own restaurant.

I'm starting my own restaurant!

THE EATER'S ARCHIVE

IT WAS WEDNESDAY MORNING at the Marrow Fair, the customers all gone, the doors closed again. Horace sidled up to my workstation while I was cleaning, and I could tell by his quiet calm—no incipient factoid, no swirling ecstasy of trivia—that something was afoot.

He lifted a loaf of the sourdough, held it at arm's length, regarded it with a new sharpness.

"You cut these faces into the crust, do you? You learned the technique from someone? From a book?"

I wiped my hands on my apron. "No," I said carefully. "I didn't learn it from a book."

"I suspected as much." He lowered his voice. "I found something."

"What kind of something?"

"What do you think?" He waggled the loaf, then tucked it under his arm like a football. "Come along." I began to protest, but he was already on his way. "Come along! You'll want to see this."

———

HE LED ME THROUGH THE LEMON GROVE and into his library, but he did not pause in the shelves. Instead, he plunged through them, and beyond, into a portal I had never before noticed—or, if I had, I assumed it led into one of the depot's innumerable dark corridors.

It did, but this corridor was lined with shelves. Horace's library continued.

"Yes, of course it does," he said. "At the time I moved here, I had two thousand linear feet of materials, and to store such a collection in archival-grade conditions . . . it was not cheap. Mr. Marrow was able to entice me primarily with the prospect of unlimited storage." He said those last words with palpable relish.

I followed him as he plunged down the corridor, which was not wide to begin with and made narrower by the shelves and legal boxes on both sides. Cold white lights above were set up on motion detectors, and they snapped to life as we approached.

As we walked, Horace's fingers danced from the lips of shelves to the lids of legal boxes. I saw annotations on the fronts of the boxes. The years ticked back like a time machine: *1992, 1991, 1990.* Horace's handwriting gave the nines long elegant tails.

Behind us, the motion-activated lights snapped off.

We passed through a tunnel of memory in a bubble of light.

"It began with a windfall," Horace said. "I used to haunt estate sales. It was my hobby. I was less focused then . . . I was interested in fin de siècle pottery, rejected applicants to the Oulipo, siege weaponry of the Gironde. But this collection that I found, it was something entirely new to me. He was a great eater, you see! John Eliot Sinclair of San Francisco. Born in 1913 and died in 1998, during that wet, wet winter, alone in his enormous house on Sacramento Street, and in the time between, he made it his mission to eat at every restaurant that opened in his city. And"—Horace turned to me, alive with astonishment—"he kept the menus. He kept all the menus!"

I didn't think you were, strictly speaking, supposed to keep the menus.

"John Eliot Sinclair must have been very charming. Or clandestine. Or both. Probably both."

"How many menus are we talking about here?"

"He was not the only one with this passion. After I acquired the Sinclair collection—for the price of hauling it away, not a penny more—I began to wonder if I hadn't stumbled onto something. The archives of the great eaters. That is what I am assembling. Here!"

He stopped short and selected a volume, fat and puffy like a photo album. He held it against the shelf and flopped it open; inside, protected by plastic overlays, were wine labels, fastidiously peeled from their bottles and flattened, each with an accompanying note written in a spidery hand. More albums waited. The wine drinker's liquid autobiography occupied four entire shelves.

When I thought of archives—documents stored and studied—I thought of poets, writers, politicians, scientists. But why shouldn't the archives of the eaters also have avid keepers?

Horace kept walking, the lights snapping on ahead of him, and I followed. The years ticked back, and around 1979, there was evidence of a transplant in process, documents being moved out of old boxes, foxed and rippled with age, into new ones, freshly assembled.

A cup from Naz's coffee bar sat on the corridor's floor beside one of the boxes.

Horace turned. "I was revisiting the Louise Bouk collection, which is of particular interest because she overlapped with John Eliot Sinclair in San Francisco. Sinclair loved the steak houses. Bouk was different; she was enthusiastic about California cuisine."

"Raw turnips drizzled in olive oil? That sort of thing?"

"I'm not sure the cuisine's adherents would call that its most soaring exponent, but yes, you have the idea. In Bouk's collection, I found . . . No, not this one . . . Where is it . . . ?"

He was pulling out menus as big as newspapers, hand-lettered and reproduced using some antique process on heavy brown paper, with fine-lined illustrations that made them look like pages from a Victorian children's book. The menus were all dated 1979.

I saw one menu titled JAPANESE DEATH POEM. Another called THE PLUM'S LAMENT. I saw a tiny, perfect sketch of a clutch of carrots with shaggy tops. Another of a very handsome goose.

Horace found his quarry. "Here," he said, offering it. "December 1979."

The menu was titled A FEAST FOR THE UNREQUITED, and it began with a dish called Sourdough à la Masque served with smoked salt and bone marrow. It was accompanied by a very respectable rendering of a loaf of bread, darkly crosshatched. The loaf was oblong and rustic and unmistakable: because a face leered out of the crust.

The name of the restaurant was written in tiny script at the bottom of the menu, almost reluctantly. I read it aloud: "Café Candide." I looked at Horace. "Have you heard of it?"

He blinked. "Yes, Lois. I have heard of it." He looked at me strangely. "Never? Truly? Perhaps . . . the Café Candide cookbooks . . . simple black covers, very elegant . . . ? She sold two million of them?"

Had I seen them at the bookstore on Clement Street? It was possible, but . . .

"Lois. Café Candide is a very important place. It is the wellspring." He shook his head. "Surely you've heard of Charlotte Clingstone."

"Is she on TV? I don't really watch—"

"I'll tell you this." Horace snorted. "You have dined, apparently without realizing it, in restaurants established by alumni of her kitchen. I know this for a fact because *all the restaurants* are established by alumni of her kitchen. It is the greatest and farthest-reaching culinary mafia since the twelve pupils of Apicius, who went out like disciples . . . Wait! You have read Everett Broom!"

The tattooed baker whose book taught me the basics of sourdough. Yes, of course.

Horace raised a finger, triumphant. "He, too, hails from the Candide clan!" Then his look grew admonishing. "Lois, it is a lazy thing not to know whose world you live in. This is Charlotte Clingstone's."

He held up the menu with its leering sourdough.

"And you see, that makes this *interesting*. Café Candide, of all places! How did a loaf with this . . . *look* arrive at Charlotte Clingstone's table? How did it come into your possession,

140

more than three decades later? Something links you to her."
He paused, as if to digest the implausibility of that statement.
"In any case, this is a highly suggestive document."

The lights above snapped off. We'd sat talking for too long.
"Does that happen often?"

"A fair amount, yes," Horace said. "I don't mind. It gives
me a minute to think."

We stayed quiet. Thinking.

"You must seek her out," Horace said at last.

He was right.

The lights snapped on again, revealing Horace on his
feet, caught mid-gesticulation. "It takes a bit of a leap to wake
them up." He straightened. "Bring the menu. I'll make you a
copy."

We walked back the way we'd come, resynchronizing with
the present.

From the disarray in the corridor, and from the bright
sticky notes affixed to the shelves and boxes and walls and
floor, overlapping in places and fluttering like feathery lichen
as we passed, it became clear: this was not a sleeping archive.
Horace had a project under way.

"What are you doing with all this?"

"I am following the path that the archive of John Eliot
Sinclair set me on. I have come to believe that food is history of
the deepest kind. Everything we eat tells a tale of ingenuity
and creation, domination and injustice—and does so more
vividly than any other artifact, any other medium. There are
histories of food, of course. I have them all here. And yet . . .
something is missing. So, I am trying to write a book."

He sighed.

"And even if I fail—this is always the archivist's consolation—perhaps I will have laid a foundation for someone wiser."

We walked farther.

"I gave this place its name, you know. I said it to Lily. I said, 'This man, our benefactor, he works powerfully in secret like a lump of marrow.' She repeated it to him, and the next thing I heard was that the place was called the Marrow Fair! And then, to his chagrin perhaps, he became Mr. Marrow. It's a wonderful word, isn't it? From the Old English *mearg*, the innermost core. The hidden heart! It makes our blood in its secret chambers. That is Mr. Marrow's ambition, I believe. The production of new blood."

The end of the corridor was in sight; across the concourse, a grow room glowed pink.

"Is he succeeding?" I asked.

"It is no small thing to change a culture," Horace said simply. "But I think interesting things are growing here. Lucrative enterprises. Provocative tastes. Perhaps, even, if you can imagine it"—he pranced into the light—"this book of mine."

Out in the concourse, among the shelves I now understood were only the tip of a vast project, Horace hunted and reached and produced a grip of books.

"Here," he said. "This is your education."

The stack contained *The Candide Cookbook* and *The Next Candide Cookbook*, both with plain black covers, along with *California Table: The Café Candide Story*, large and glossy, and finally a floppy paperback titled *Tend Your Garden: Charlotte Clingstone and the Making of a Perfect Place*.

That last volume showed on its cover a woman, broad-faced and serene, standing in a garden wearing very comfortable pants. A sense of recognition circled the runway, came in to land: I knew Charlotte Clingstone after all. She had been part of the panel at the Ferry Building. She was the central deity. *That will be all.* I had no doubt: she was the one who'd said no.

I N YOUR MESSAGE, you told me about your family, how you don't have any traditions. The first time I read that, it made me sad, but then I thought about it for a while and I started to feel jealous. Lois, think about it! No one cares if your restaurant has tables. You can build robots, or bake bread, or do something else entirely. You're unencumbered by culture. You're . . . light!

We've arrived in Berlin. This apartment is bigger than the last one, but it's really dark. Shehrieh says it's fine. I still haven't told her about my restaurant.

Chaiman wants me to tell you he misses your city by the bay. As for me, I miss your voice on the phone.

THE LOIS CLUB (CONTINUED)

I'D SKIPPED A MEETING of the Lois Club, not because I consciously decided not to go, but because I'd been so busy it had escaped me completely. I sent an apology to Hilltop Lois a week late and promised I had not forsaken them. *We missed your bread!!!!* she replied. She seemed to use more exclamation marks every time.

When I entered, bearing six loaves of bread—one to eat, the rest to distribute as gifts—the Loises all fell silent. I'd expected a hero's welcome; instead, they looked at me strangely.

"What?"

"It's just—you look so different," Professor Lois said.

"You look wonderful!" Compaq Lois said.

"Do I really look that different? What do you mean?"

"You just—" Professor Lois searched for words. "You're in great shape. Have you been doing yoga?"

"You're making us feel bad!" Old Lois cackled. "Here we are, all the same as ever. Of course, for some of us, that's an achievement . . ."

To fill the silence, I started to unspool the story of the last month. They didn't know about the Marrow Fair. I told them everything.

"Can I shop there?" Compaq Lois asked. "It sounds fabulous."

I explained that it ran previews early on Wednesday mornings, but by invitation only, and that it would be opening to everyone soon.

"And you're going to Café Candide?" Professor Lois asked. "How wonderful. My husband and I went there years ago. Our twentieth wedding anniversary."

"Hope you saved your pennies," Old Lois said. "I hear it's pricey."

"I'm not going to eat," I said. "Just to investigate."

"I saw her speak at the Commonwealth Club," Professor Lois said. "Charlotte Clingstone. Very impressive woman."

"I saw her in a documentary on KQED," Hilltop Lois interjected.

"I met her at a fund-raiser," Compaq Lois said. "For the turkey vultures."

They had started and it seemed they couldn't stop. Their fascination surprised me; but as they spoke—

"She spent three years in France, you know."

—I realized—

"Yes, she met her husband there."

—Charlotte Clingstone presented a kind of ideal. She was bohemian but accomplished. Worldly but rooted.

"Her *first* husband. Now she's married to a poet."

Who wouldn't want that life?

"Oh, yes. I have his book. He dedicated it to her."

"That was his first one. The second, he dedicated to her plums."

"Her plums!"

"No, he really meant it. In the back, in the garden behind the restaurant, I guess there's this amazing plum tree . . ."

"Her *plums*," Old Lois crowed.

"I'll see if I can spot the tree tomorrow," I said.

"Yes," Old Lois said between snorts. She couldn't stop laughing. "Watch for those plums!"

THE HUB, THE HEART

SAN FRANCISCO IS SHORT ON GREENERY and the streets
have a bare brightness. Berkeley runs wilder. Walking
from the North Berkeley BART station to Café Candide, I had
to circle around huge hedges that surged and blocked the
sidewalk. There were no lawns. Instead, residents cultivated
behemoth planter boxes; personal citrus groves; gardens of
meaty succulents that seemed to glow with an inner light.
The streets were quiet, but I sensed eyes through gauzy cur-
tains. A fat squirrel shadowed me for a block.

In one place, a massive willow tree's roots had split the
pavement. Its leaves brushed my head.

I pulled out my phone to double-check the restaurant's
address, but I didn't have to search for it: Café Candide was
preemptively inscribed on the map, like a government office
or a natural landmark.

When I emerged into the quiet shopping district I saw the
rim of the hills looming above, a dark cutout now turning
pink in the evening light, the steep wooded slope crusted
with houses whose windows flashed white in the sun.

I found the restaurant smashed between a hardware store and a mobile phone outlet peddling a brand I didn't recognize. Both store and outlet looked like they belonged on this block; Café Candide, not so much. That impression was wrong, of course. Café Candide had stood here for decades while businesses flashed through the storefronts on both sides.

It was a house of darkest gingerbread, odd-angled and enormous, seeming to lean slightly on its neighbors. Yes, Berkeley Nuts-n-Bolts and Air Zero were definitely providing significant structural support to the old restaurant. Café Candide's roof was densely shingled and sharply slanted. A short chimney tossed up a ragged streamer of smoke.

It was very clearly a witch's abode.

The house/restaurant was set back from the sidewalk, guarded by a stubby fence of wrought iron, the gate currently open. My heels *thwapped* across a patio paved in slate. The door was a slab of dark wood with an iron handle that matched the fence. The wood was carved with a mazelike pattern; I wanted to plunk my finger down and find my way through it. The maze's channels shone smooth and glossy, so maybe I wasn't the first person to feel that impulse.

There was no sign that said CAFÉ CANDIDE. There was also no doubt that this was the place.

I knocked, or tried. My best effort produced barely any sound; it was like knocking on a mattress. So I took the door by its handle, hauled it open a crack, and before it could close again, I slithered through.

Inside, a young woman in a linen smock was pushing a mop across gleaming floorboards. The soap smelled dense and spicy.

"Excuse me," I said. Her eyes snapped up. "I'm here to see Charlotte Clingstone. I called this morning."

The smocked mopper nodded and beckoned for me to follow.

She glided through the cool, dark dining room. The tables and chairs matched the paneling on the walls and the boards beneath my feet; the room could have been carved from one great block of wood. Everything was soft and smooth, polished by use. I saw myself reflected in the floor. A warm shadow.

The smocked mopper led me through a swinging door into the kitchen.

According to Horace, this was it. The hub, the heart. Sanctum sanctorum. The quiet workers before me—currently chopping, cleaning, carving, prepping, planning, all in matching smocks—would in time open restaurants, host TV shows, write bestselling cookbooks. I had penetrated the innermost crèche of California cuisine.

Where, as in Chef Kate's kitchen, hip-hop was playing on a whoomphy Bluetooth speaker.

The smocked mopper glided through the kitchen and I followed her path as precisely as I could, wary of getting in anyone's way. I kept my head down.

Then I saw the oven.

It was epic, with a pale stone dome, walls of black-lacquered brick, and a yawning mouth with a flicking, forking tongue of fire. The heat was palpable from across the kitchen. As I passed, a red-faced baker twirled a long wooden paddle—her arms were enormous—and sent it slicing into the oven to slip beneath two loaves at once. With a snap of her shoulders they were out, rough and crackly, uppermost edges singed black. Her bread looked even more rustic than Everett Broom's, like some primordial ancestor from a harder epoch—one that required more armor. As I watched, she dropped the loaves into a line that was forming on the counter-top, then gave the paddle another twirl, tossing it into the air as she did, a confident flourish intended for no one but herself.

"Awwwesommmc." I groaned it out loud without intending to. She heard me, and a wicked grin flashed across her face.

I spotted the baker's starter sitting on the countertop in a widemouthed plastic tub. Its name was written on a band of peeling tape: CLINT YEASTWOOD.

The smocked mopper waited at the next door, impatient with my awe. I followed into a dark hallway lined with coats on pegs and shoes and boots on the floor, past a small wash-room, around a corner.

We came to a door, slightly ajar. The smocked mopper knocked gently, and when the reply came—a crisp command to enter—she left me to discover on my own what waited within.

THE ROOM WAS LONG AND SKINNY, set up against the back of the building, with tall windows that offered a panoramic view of the restaurant's backyard garden filtered through a veil of beans that climbed lengths of string pulled taut across the windows, their leaves softening the light that fell into the study.

Through the beans, I saw figures moving in the garden, filling baskets with greens. More acolytes, serene in their linen smocks.

At a small desk, Charlotte Clingstone sat in dappled bean-shadow. Before her were a laptop, an enormous pile of documents, and not one but three phones. She was poking at one of them as I entered. She glanced up with a look of annoyance.

It was definitely her: the central deity from the Ferry Building.

"Someone named Lawrence," I said. "I talked to him on the phone . . . He said you would have time to see me. Around now."

"Lawrence is very accommodating," Clingstone said. She lowered her glasses and a look of recognition flitted across her face. "I know you. How do I know you?"

I hadn't expected her to recognize me, but maybe the fact that I had presented her pantheon with something other than pickles had earned me a single sparking neuron.

I told her I was Lois Clary. I'd tried out for the Bay Area farmers markets . . . all of them . . . and been rejected.

"Oh, I hope you're not here about that." Pity and impatience mixed in her voice. She fiddled with her phones, moving them into a neat line. I wondered if she had a panic button mounted on the underside of her desk to call for help in case of confrontation by spurned farmers and/or simpering gourmands.

"I came to show you something." I crossed the distance between us and extracted the copy of Horace's menu from my bag. "This."

She hitched her glasses up and peered at the menu. "Goodness."

"Do you remember it?"

"Well, give me a moment." Her eyes flitted across the

paper. "I've made quite a few of these, you know. Hmm . . . 1979. This is ancient." Her eyes scanned farther down, and something crossed her face. A softening. "Oh, yes. I do remember." She looked up at me. "Where did you find this?"

"A friend of mine. Horace, he's a—"

"Portacio. Of course." She clucked. "It's quite a hoard he's gathered. I didn't know I was part of it."

"He has all your cookbooks, too."

"A lot of people have my cookbooks. No one has these menus anymore. I wish I did."

"I wanted to ask you about something specific. About this meal."

"Go on."

"The bread. Sourdough à la Masque. What was it? Where did it come from?"

Outside, the acolytes moved in the garden.

"It's the most interesting thing on the menu, isn't it?" Clingstone mused. "I don't think that's obvious. Am I remembering correctly—you're a baker? Yes, I can see why you might be curious about this. Well. All right."

She stood, slipped a manila folder under her arm, dropped a phone into each of her jacket's pockets, leaving the third on the table. "Come along, then. I'll explain."

She led me out through the warren—past the washroom, the coats—and back into the kitchen, where it was a different thing entirely to enter in the presence of Charlotte Clingstone. Nothing outwardly changed—not one knife skipped a chop—but a crackling field of attention snapped into existence.

"Where's Lawrence?" Clingstone called out. "Someone find Lawrence, please. His memory is required."

Acolytes zipped out every door.

Clingstone glided over to the burly baker. "Mona," she said sweetly. The baker glowed. Clingstone turned to me. "This is Lois. She bakes."

Mona's gaze cooled. I was an intruder in her domain.

Clingstone lifted one of the loaves from the line, tapped it on its back. "Lovely," she cooed. She returned it to the line and lowered her glasses. "I've always thought the starter's influence was overstated. People tell these wild stories— 'Oh, I got it from such-and-such, it's been going strong since, you know, Sister Brunhilde began it in Gothenburg a hundred years ago,' that sort of thing—but it's all basically the same."

"I agree," Mona said. As if she had any choice.

"But," Clingstone said, "there *was* an exception. Years ago. Look at this." She handed Mona the menu I'd brought. "From 1979, you see? We were just starting. This was still Harriet Grayling's house, and we were her wild young friends"—Clingstone seemed to apply some retroactive skepticism to this—"throwing these enormous dinners in her parlor. This kitchen was different. It was tiny." She snapped her head around. "*Where* is Lawrence? I need him to remember something."

Two more acolytes went scurrying.

She turned back to Mona and me. "It was becoming a bit of a flophouse. Harriet didn't mind. She was having the time of her life. It was that summer, I think, when Jim Bascule wandered through. A friend of someone's . . . I can't remember who. Lawrence!"

Another acolyte gone.

"He'd been in Europe. He'd met someone. They'd lived

together in Brussels. She was a wonderful cook, apparently. She baked bread. He fell in love. Then she left, and he ran out of money. He showed up here with nothing but a beat-up old guitar and the sourdough starter she'd left behind."

Around the kitchen, those acolytes who had not gone in search of Clingstone's quarry tilted themselves to hear the story. This was precious history. Indoctrination.

"Jim Bascule played his guitar all day, singing sad songs. He might have been in a band. I can't remember. I need Lawrence! But"—she clucked—"here was the surprise. Every morning, Jim baked. His lady had taught him well. The bread was wonderful, but also . . ." She paused. Looked from Mona to me with eyes that dared us to question what came next. "There's no getting around it, is there? There were faces in the crust. These strange . . . sharp-edged . . ." She curled her fingers and made a face. An ecstatic mask. I recognized the spirit of it immediately. Her features returned to normal. "We ignored them. Those weren't the strangest things we saw back then. Jim baked that bread every day for . . . six months? We paid him what we could. He saved it all up, until he had enough for a ticket back to Europe."

Mona was fully caught up in the story. "To go after his lady?"

"That was the idea. We threw him a going-away party." She held up the menu: A FEAST FOR THE UNREQUITED. "Back then, we could get away with names like this." She smiled and was lost for a moment. "Someone—I can't remember who; where's Lawrence? He knows all these things—someone tried to keep the starter alive, but it just . . ." Clingstone made a limp gesture. "We all said it died of a broken heart."

An acolyte burst into the kitchen trailing a man, wiry and bald, Clingstone's age, cradling a bottle of wine under each arm.

"*There* you are!" Clingstone cried.

His hair rose up in a frizzy halo around his skull. "What is it, my love?"

"I needed you for a story. But now I'm done with it. Do you remember Jim Bascule?"

"I certainly remember Jim Bascule's *bread*, darling."

Clingstone offered the man the old menu for his inspection. He leaned close, and while his eyes scanned the page, she said to me, "This is my husband, Lawrence. Although he wasn't my husband when this menu was written."

Lawrence looked up and said drily, "I was only her lover then."

"In any case," Clingstone said, "I haven't thought about that bread in years. It was wonderful."

It was clear that Mona, the baker, would have preferred for this story to be recounted to her exclusively. She addressed me. "You're a professional? Do you work for Broom, or . . . ?"

Here I was at the wellspring, the source, and this baker was checking my credentials—her curious gaze joined by Clingstone's now, and Lawrence's—and I wanted to impress them.

"I'm the baker at the Marrow Fair," I said. "The market on Alameda. Have you—?"

Charlotte Clingstone's expression closed like a gate crashing down. She started to speak, but only made a clucking sound. Currents of annoyance swirled across her face.

"The Marrow Fair," Lawrence repeated, trying the name on for size. "Do you know it, darling?"

"I do," Clingstone said. "I've heard about it. From Portacio, and others."

"Ah, Horace!"

"He's my friend," I said. "He found this menu." For Lawrence's benefit, I explained: "It's a new kind of market."

"Very . . . forward-thinking," Clingstone said lightly. Other possible adjectives played across her lips. "Its founder thinks our restaurant here is quite retrograde. Even a bit silly."

I felt waves of opprobrium from the acolytes. If Clingstone ordered them to beat me to death with rolling pins and stale sourdough, there could be no doubt: they would do it.

I sputtered, "I'm sure he doesn't. I mean. I don't really know anything about him. I only make bread. I have a robot."

Mona looked at me with pity.

One of the phones in Clingstone's pocket buzzed. She peeked at the screen and said, "I'm sorry. I'm late for a call." Retreating back into the warren of the restaurant, she paused a moment, then turned. Her gaze was chilly and complex. "Now I wish I hadn't told you that story."

Lawrence escorted me out of Café Candide, and, on the way through the dining room, he swiped a bottle from inside a white cardboard box. "Take this to Horace. He'll like it. Sorry about Charlotte. Well, not really. This Marrow Fair place sounds wretched." He said it with winning diffidence. "But it's all changing, isn't it? No matter. We'll stay the same. You should come for dinner sometime. We have tables available next spring, I believe."

<FROM: BEO>

I T'S STRANGE TO HEAR the starter might have reached San Francisco once before! Mainly I'm surprised it wasn't a Mazg who brought it. Actually, I think I might be a little bit scandalized. Who was this Jim Bascule guy?

Chaiman finished his album. It has seven tracks and he calls it *The Mazg Tapes.* I don't think he's ever touched a tape in his life. Shehrieh is super worried about it—she doesn't want him to use the word "Mazg"—and that is *very* good news for me. I told her about my restaurant and she barely blinked. Sorry, Chaiman!

I'll attach the album. I like some of the tracks more than others (it gets *oonce*-y . . .), but mostly, I'm proud of my brother for making something that's truly his.

BOONVILLE

THE EXPEDIENT SEARCH ENGINE revealed that Jim Bascule had, sometime between the mid-1970s and today, become a winemaker in Mendocino County. On the website for a winery called Tradecraft, I found his picture. He looked to be in his sixties, scruffy at the chin, blond hair gone gray curling down to his shoulders. There might be more than one Jim Bascule in the world, but this image reassured me. He looked like the kind of person who might have taken up residence at a turnip restaurant in Berkeley.

The drive was long, three hours. I listened to the radio until the signal faded and then switched to Chaiman's Mazg remix album, which steadily increased in tempo as it proceeded from track to track. When it got to be too much, the sad Mazg voices all warped into the chipmunk register, I stopped the album short and went back to the beginning, where it was slower, with undistorted crooning buoyed by a spare accompaniment, which seemed to fit the landscape better.

Fog became mist, which accumulated in sheets on my windshield. I drove very, very slowly, occasionally pulling into turnouts to allow pickup trucks to roar past me, sending up high plumes behind them. My car moaned pitifully as I crawled over a steep switchbacking rise, then coasted with palpable relief down a long and lazy slope toward my destination.

Boonville was a short strip of shops and restaurants huddled along California State Route 128 where it dropped into the golden fold of Anderson Valley. There were wineries on both sides of the road, some with ramshackle tasting rooms. The local brewery maintained a hopyard, pale buds clinging to long wires parallel to the road. I passed a broad-faced hotel that seemed to preside over the tiny town. I thought about stopping. Maybe on the way back.

My phone had no signal here, but it had already loaded the map I needed and my GPS showed the way. I turned off the highway onto a hard-packed dirt road, now mottled with puddles, and followed it for a mile until I saw a wooden sign for TRADECRAFT.

The driveway plunged through the scrim of eucalyptus and dipped to cross a wide bridge over a rushing creek. The planks went *thump-thump-thump* beneath my tires. My car's engine groaned a little as I pushed it crunching onto a gravel parking lot. There were two other vehicles parked there in the rain.

The winery was a long building with a log-cabin look. A small sign advertised the tasting room. Inside, I found a middle-aged woman sitting on a stool behind a countertop, absorbed in a Thomas Pynchon novel. She set it aside when she saw me.

"Welcome to Tradecraft! Not the nicest day for wine tasting, is it? Anyone else, or just you?"

I told her I was alone, and that I was here to see Jim Bascule.

"He just went to drop a couple cases off at the hotel. He'll be back soon. Can I offer you a taste while you wait? I'm Barbara."

I acquiesced, peeled off my jacket, and set it down with my tote bag containing a loaf of bread. (I was always carrying bread these days.) I sipped samples of three red wines and two whites as Barbara probed me gently, learning that I lived in San Francisco ("I love the city") and worked as a programmer ("Is everyone a computer person now? It seems that way") but also baked bread ("Have you been to the bakery across from the hotel? They make the best scones. The *best*"), and I had, in fact, brought a loaf for Jim Bascule.

"How nice! Well, he should be back any minute. Let's finish with this, the Tradecraft Gewürz. It's what we're known for."

She uncorked a slender bottle and poured a trickle into a narrow glass. The wine shimmered thickly.

"Have you heard of botrytis?" She said the word carefully, *bo-try-tis*. "They call it the 'noble rot.' These grapes actually get moldy on the vine. On purpose, I mean. It gives the wine a flavor—you'll see."

I took a sip. The wine felt heavy in my mouth. It was very sweet but also tartly acidic, and the taste lingered for a long time. Barbara poured a glass for herself, nearly full-size, and her eyes were closed when she lifted it to her lips.

We were both quiet, sipping, when I felt a draft of cold, wet air. Barbara's eyes fluttered open. "There he is!"

JIM BASCULE WAS SHORT AND LEAN, a sixty-year-old man with the bearing of a boy. His chin bristled with blond whiskers and his hair was pulled away from his shoulders into a neat ponytail.

I introduced myself and he shook my hand, looking plainly puzzled.

"Are you the Jim Bascule who baked at Café Candide?"

His eyebrows leapt. "I'm not sure if I am . . . But I remember him, sure. How do you know about that?"

As explanation, I hauled my tote bag onto the countertop, drew out the loaf of bread, and thumped it down.

He looked first at me, then at the bread. He smiled. And, of course, the bread smiled back.

I followed him out of the tasting room into a cluttered kitchen. Cases of wine were stacked haphazardly. There were also miscellaneous wheels of cheese and thin sausages hanging on strings like torpid bats. A slab of wood supported an array of jams as well as what appeared to be a loaf of bread, its brown bottom peeking out from underneath a towel patterned with blue flowers.

Bascule swept the towel back. The loaf underneath was round and thick-crusted with a burnish to shame Everett Broom. That crust didn't show a face, but instead an intricate spiral.

"Did you do that yourself?" I asked.

"I think you know I didn't," Bascule said.

Here's what he told me.

When he was preparing to reunite with his love in Europe—or so he thought—Jim Bascule left the starter with his parents in Santa Rosa, and he shared with them his suspicion: that it needed music to flourish.

"Things didn't work out in Brussels," he said. "Oh, gosh. She lived in this little apartment overlooking an alley . . . she had a balcony where she grew herbs. She knew everyone, and she was always helping people. Little favors, and big ones, too. I was smitten. There's no question I built her up in my mind while I was away. By the time I returned, she'd met someone else. This gorgeous Greek guy. I didn't stand a chance. So I wandered a bit, got involved in some other things."

What kind of things?

"Oh, things. I didn't come back to the States until 1985. When I returned, I discovered my dad still had the starter going. That whole time"—Bascule started to laugh—"he'd been playing it the Grateful Dead!"

So here I was seeing the hippie spiraling crust of a Deadhead starter.

"I still play it the Dead every night. There's a lot of bootlegs."

But how? Why?

"Here's my theory, honed over decades of bullshitting to myself. This starter, it uses music as a kind of . . . synchronization. It helps the little yeasts and whatever-elses to do the right things at the right times. You've gotta be careful, though."

Careful how?

Bascule laughed drily. "I used to play around with other music, just to see. You know that classical tune 'Flight of the Bumblebee'?" He whistled a bit of the breakneck melody. "I left it alone for fifteen minutes, no more. When I came back inside, it had spilled out of its container. It was *everywhere*." He eyed me sharply. "You seen anything like that with yours?"

I confessed I hadn't. The Clement Street starter was well behaved.

"Well, be careful. I think the music matters. After that happened, I thought I'd finally killed it. Stuff barely bubbled for weeks. Now I just play it the Dead. Good vibes."

I traced my finger around the maze, an inch above the sourdough's crust. "Don't you find this . . . really exceptionally strange?"

Bascule shrugged. "I've done a bit of reading. The way these things work together . . . It's unbelievable. I'm sure you've heard all this stuff about the bacteria in our gut, how they're like a second brain? There's a lab—this was just published recently—there's a lab where they've got some yeasts hooked up to the internet. You can log in and reprogram their DNA."

That sounded like a terrible idea.

"My point is, there are things in this living world plenty weirder than this. If you want proof, just come back and visit us in the fall. See the grapes."

"The ones with the fungus?"

"You ever heard of a suitcase clone? No? Well, okay. Come back in the fall."

Before I left the winery, I asked one last question.

"Who was she? The woman in Belgium who gave you the starter?"

Bascule shook his head. "She had the strangest name."

ON THE WAY OUT OF TOWN, I stopped at the Boonville Hotel. Inside, I walked down a shadowed hall to claim a stool at the short bar—I was the only one there—and when the bartender appeared, who was also the hotel's manager, I ordered a glass of the Tradecraft Gewürtztraminer.

Through an open doorway, I watched a small kitchen staff working quietly, preparing that evening's meal. I wondered how one of General Dexterity's robot arms—with kitchen skills!—would fit in here on the side of California State Route 128. Would it ruin that kitchen, or improve it? I genuinely didn't know.

I sipped my wine slowly.

I pondered the egg problem.

I wondered what other music I could play for the Clement Street starter. Was there any album, any composition, that would encourage a crust that looked simply . . . normal?

The bartender/manager came back out and asked me if I'd be joining them for dinner. I asked him what they were serving, and he reported: roasted chicken, accompanied by a panzanella salad with tomatoes from the garden and croutons from homemade sourdough.

I told him I had to get back to the office.

<FROM: BEO>

YOU SHOULD HAVE SEEN my mother's face when Chaiman and I asked her about Jim Bascule. She told us she hadn't thought of that name in thirty-some years.

Apparently, when he appeared again in Brussels, Shehrieh was shocked. She refused him, and she told us she felt bad about it, but he was too short, and he couldn't cook anything. Well, he could bake bread, but she'd taught him that. And there was another man, he was Greek . . . this was before Leopold. (My father wasn't home when we were talking about all this, and I think that was probably for the best.)

But I understand what she means about the cooking. It's crucial in Mazg relationships, especially in the beginning. How do you even get started if you can't woo the other person with your spicy soup?

THAT WASN'T A EUPHEMISM!

THE EGG PROBLEM

D URING MY SENIOR YEAR OF COLLEGE, at the urging of a professor who specialized in the history of the assembly line, I had embarked on a self-directed project to identify the first use of a computer program in a manufacturing process. After a semester of digging through libraries in East Lansing and Ann Arbor, I had scrounged a few early examples, but I failed to convince either Evelyn Simmons or myself that I had succeeded in my task. Nevertheless, she gave me a 4.0 and told me I'd learned a useful skill.

I used it now.

I was going to be the one to solve the egg problem.

I read up on anatomy and physiology. I acquired textbooks for students of physical therapy and DVDs for students of dance. I tracked down software from a company called Anatomix that could accurately simulate the flex of skin and muscle, and I inspected every menu, every command. Horace became my research assistant: he scoured the internet and brought me three new kinesiology papers every day; dropped them on the countertop still warm from the laser printer.

Sometimes, when I was sitting at the long picnic table

reading and rereading the papers, sipping endless cappuccinos provided by Naz, I paused to wonder: Who paid for all this?

The master of the market, the figure known universally as Mr. Marrow, was an enigma. Horace hypothesized that our patron was the scion of an old San Francisco family that had earned its fortune feeding the Barbary Coast. Naz was more paranoid, and said Mr. Marrow walked among us. "He could be Horace, for all we know." I heard from others that Mr. Marrow was obviously Anthony Bourdain; definitely Ferran Adrià; indisputably Sergey Brin.

Every day, I carried a carton from the open pantry and placed it before the Vitruvian. One by one, it lifted the eggs, and one by one, it ruined them.

I imagined Mr. Marrow looking at a rapidly growing outlay for pasture-raised eggs and wondering, *What the—?*

I had watched the Vitruvian make a hundred attempts without any apparent improvement. At the Task Acquisition Center, identical arms had ruined probably thousands of eggs. (What happened to those eggs? Did we, the Dextrous, eat them as breakfast scrambles? I hoped we did.) The problem wasn't the training. There was something about this task that eluded ArmOS, even when it had mastered so many others. It could assemble a phone, but it couldn't open an egg.

Could I criticize it, really? My own egg-cracking experience was extremely limited—a cookie-baking spree during my senior year of college; everything but the egg and a little butter was already in the box—and in that time I had certainly never attempted to do it one-handed, which was what was required of the Vitruvian. Even with the benefit of two hands, my egg-cracking had been fumbling, borderline disastrous—a gentle rain of eggshell into the cookie mix, shards removed carefully one by one.

If I was going to have any hope of teaching the Vitruvian, I would have to master this skill myself.

I opened the expedient video-sharing website on my laptop, searched for "how to crack an egg," and was rewarded with thousands of results. I selected the first and watched a disembodied hand crack an egg against the rim of a clear glass bowl and pull its halves apart, two fingers forward, two fingers back. The gesture was almost obscenely elegant. I tried to copy what I saw on the screen, and was rewarded with a smear of yolk across my palm.

I felt a surge of kinship with the Vitruvian. We were starting at the same level.

But there was a difference between us: I learned fast.

Thwack, crack, pull—after only a few attempts, I could do it as neatly as my faceless tutor. *Thwack, crack, pull.* There's a technical term for this: "one-shot learning." You see something once; you can do it. Programmers who work on artificial intelligence and robot locomotion regard it with nearly mystical awe.

Having mastered the elegant, one-handed egg-crack in if not one, then maybe three shots, I set myself to the deeper task of understanding it. I pushed all my awareness into my hands—muscles, tendons, finger pads. *Thwack, crack, pull.* *Thwack, crack* . . . another smear. As quickly as I had learned it, I unlearned it. *Thwack* . . . The egg didn't even crack. My fingers trembled.

I repeated this cycle every afternoon for a week. Every session contained, at its peak, a few perfect, satisfying cracks, with the broken shell levered apart by the subtlest workings of my fingers and palm. But the sessions all ended the same way, with me so lost in amped-up self-awareness—proprioception!—that I was dinging the eggs harmlessly off the bowl, or demolishing them entirely, just like the Vitruvian. Our performance converged. I had nothing to teach it.

After this happened, I would angrily dispose of the broken eggs, feeling stupid and wasteful, then stomp up and down the concourse in frustration.

And I would watch other people work.

When Naz used his espresso machine, it was musical: *clack* of portafilter, *hiss* of steam, *gurgle* of milk, *clink* of saucer. When Anita worked her cricket flour into dough, she stared into space, thinking with her hands. That's what I wanted to achieve. Even Jaina Mitra: when she shuttled samples between her great microbial menagerie and the DNA sequencer, her fingers and feet moved of their own accord. *She* was elsewhere, gaze clouded, brain churning. She could have done it with her eyes closed.

That, of course, was it.

I ran back to my workstation, opened my laptop, and made sure I was synchronized with the latest changes to ArmOS. It was going to be so simple. It was going to be so huge.

To date, my contributions to the codebase had all been tiny refinements—painstaking embroideries in the tight tapestry of Proprioception. I had also written a related debugging panel for Interface, but I would never admit to that.

Now I created a module from whole cloth. It was concise, not even a hundred lines of code, built in perfect symmetry around a single action. One by one, in exactly the right order, I suspended the arm's motor control loops. Then I loaded the action directly into the PKD 2891 Stepper Motors, which most people didn't realize you could do; they all had their own MCUs, with just enough memory for what came next. Then, one by one, I brought the motor control loops back online.

I finished my new module, named it, tried to compile, was informed of several embarrassing syntax errors, corrected them, compiled again. I flashed the Vitruvian with the new code and said aloud, "Try again."

It plucked up an egg, moved it lightly into position, paused, and *thwack*ed the egg against the rim of the bowl. Just after the *thwack*, my new module took over. The motor control loops went dark. The arm wasn't running blind; it was more like . . . a blink. Not even a hundred milliseconds, during which my new module said: *Just go for it.*

In the ArmOS codebase, as part of the Control package, I had created something new—a tiny space without feedback or self-awareness—and I had named it Confidence.

The yolk flowed out with the albumen while the shell came apart cleanly in the Vitruvian's six-fingered grip. The arm swiveled and dropped the shell neatly into the small bowl I had set up for that purpose—the bowl that had never before this moment actually been needed.

I had solved the egg problem, and I had done so in the simplest way possible: not by adding code, but by taking it away. During the blink, the Vitruvian was no longer caught in a wash of continuous feedback. It was no longer second-guessing its second guesses a thousand times every second.

I bundled my new module into a pull request and sent it upstream, straight into the master branch of ArmOS. I didn't even write a commit message. The module's name would suffice. I waited for the emails. My heart was pounding.

"Do that again," I told the Vitruvian.

Thwack, crack, pull.

My laptop pinged. It was a message from Peter, composed entirely of exclamation marks.

Confidence!

ELEPHANTS' ARMPITS

HORACE'S E-NEWSLETTER brought with it a schedule of classes—the expertise of the Marrow Fair shared freely. Aeroponics with Kenyatta on Monday; cheese tasting with Orli on Tuesday; bug husbandry with Anita on Thursday; and on Friday, Jaina Mitra would teach a workshop on DNA sequencing.

I recruited Horace and we went together.

A very small group gathered at noon in the center of Jaina Mitra's lab. Naz from the coffee bar was there, as well as Clay from NewBagel, and Kenyatta, one of the pink-light farmers.

Jaina Mitra offered a plastic dish. "Who wants to spit?"

Horace raised his hand and expectorated neatly.

"Okay," Jaina Mitra said. "So there's a whole lot of things living in a human mouth, and we might want to know what they are. You want to know, don't you, Mr. Portacio?"

"You have no idea!"

"Biologists have become very interested in *communities* of microorganisms," Jaina Mitra said. "Characterizing the community in a sample like this used to be a laborious process, but now—watch."

Her machine was enormous, as big as a refrigerator, with a round-cornered plastic carapace, glossy white with black accents. A line of letters on the front edge named it the ILLUMINA HYPER CENSUS.

Jaina Mitra pressed a button on its belly and the machine released a tray. She laid the dish of Horace's spit into place, and when she pressed the button again, the machine pulled the tray back into itself and began to hum.

"What's it doing?" Naz asked.

"First, it denatures the sample. It heats the microbes up to make them . . . relax. Then it mashes them up using tiny beads. It's quite a massacre."

I raised a finger. "Won't that mix all the different DNA together?"

"Yes, but they can't hide. Organisms share a lot of genes, but there's one that's unique between species. Sixteen-S. It's like a fingerprint." Jaina Mitra grinned wolfishly. "So we'll pick through the body parts to find the fingertips."

We all thought about that for a moment while the machine whomped and whirred.

"While it's mashing," Jaina Mitra said, "I'll show you my collection."

She led us to an enormous refrigerated cabinet stocked with trays, each holding dozens of tiny vials.

"This is why I came here," Jaina Mitra said proudly. "Mr. Marrow promised me a subscription to the Global Microbiome Survey. It's not cheap."

Horace, gravitationally attracted to collections of all kinds, put his face up against the glass. "What do you have in there?"

"Environmental samples. The National Science Foundation sends students all over the world. I did it one summer in grad school. It's a bit of a boondoggle, really. You pick the wildest place you can imagine. I went to Greenland."

"You went to Greenland . . . on purpose," Naz said.

"It was very interesting, microbially. I sent back huge tubs"—she circled her arms around an imaginary barrel—"full of ice and mud. Rainwater, too."

"So this is a catalog of puddles," Horace said. His breath was fogging up the glass.

"Among other things. There's a bit of the Great Lakes in there. The Great Pacific Garbage Patch. Swamps. Volcanoes. There are samples scraped out of caves, and birds' nests, and elephants' armpits. New samples are coming in constantly. I just got one from an Arby's in Clearwater, Florida."

We all shuddered.

"How many labs have a subscription like this?" I asked.

"Thirty, thirty-five? Like I said, it's not cheap."

"What do you *do* with it?"

Jaina Mitra's face took on a hungry look. "Think of it as raw genetic ore. All the subscribers are on a mailing list. When a lab identifies a new species, they send out an alert. I just heard that an organism in the Mono Lake sample has some interesting enzymatic regulation properties, so I'm going to see if I can isolate it and—" The sequencing machine interrupted with a low and commanding chime. "Oh, here we go." Jaina Mitra tilted the laptop beside the Illumina Hyper Census.

"Anyway," she said, "let's hope Mr. Portacio's saliva isn't as mysterious as those samples." On the laptop's screen, she swiped the cursor with the ease of long practice, summoning the machine's results.

Horace frowned. "I expect it to be strange and wondrous."

On the screen, a spiky line appeared, utterly unremark-able. It could have been the price of a stock or the tempera-ture in a midwestern city. Then another layer of information arrived: a label for each of the spikes.

Jaina Mitra read them off: "*Veillonella . . . Prevotella . . . Porphyromonas gingivalis*, but not too much. Oh, and *Strep-tococcus*. That's what gives you strep throat, but it's also what they use to make Swiss cheese. You have a very healthy oral microbiome, Mr. Portacio."

Horace looked disappointed.

Kenyatta was growing agitated. "I don't understand how you use this information," he said. The tone of his voice indi-cated he did, in fact, have his suspicions, and he didn't like them.

"My work is all about microbial communities," Jaina Mitra said. "If you want to know how your plants are doing, you need to look at them, right? This is how I look at my communities."

He narrowed his eyes. "So you're just reading DNA. Not editing it."

Jaina Mitra pursed her lips. "I've experimented with CRISPR protocols, of course. Those colonies all collapsed, but—"

"Seriously?" he sputtered. "You need to come *here* to do that?" He clutched his head and walked in a little circle. Disbelief. "I thought this place was supposed to be for *new* ideas, but, I don't know, Dr. Mitra, this sounds a lot like the same old GMO shit."

"It's really not—"

"Did you get rejected from DuPont, or what? No? Maybe you should take this there. They'd be all over it."

"You have a problem with Lembas," Jaina Mitra said flatly, "but I'm not sure what it is."

"This approach—everything you're doing, the *scanning*, the *editing*—it's the height of hubris. Like, the *height*. Look around. I'm sorry if it sounds mean, but, we—don't—need you—to work on this. The plants are way, way ahead of you, Dr. Mitra. Do you *really* think—"

"Mr. Marrow supports my project."

Kenyatta snorted. "I wonder what he'd say if I told him it was either your lab or our grow rooms. We make half of the food that goes out the door here." He started to stomp away, then caught himself and turned back, made a final plea. "I'm no traditionalist. I mean, pink LEDs—come on. But there's a difference, right? Plants have developed over millions of years. They just *work*. What you're doing—it's not natural."

Jaina Mitra clicked her tongue. "Nothing is natural."

AFTER THE SEQUENCING SESSION WAS OVER, I walked with Horace through the grove at the heart of the concourse.

"These are Meyer lemons," Horace said as we passed the trees. "Named for Frank Nicholas Meyer. Dutch by birth, but an agent of the United States government. He worked for the Department of Agriculture's Office of Seed and Plant Introduction before the First World War. I thought of him when Jaina Mitra spoke of her microbial survey. Meyer and his cohort were hunters for larger prey. They canvassed the world and sent back living samples of plants thought to be useful to the advancement of the American economy. Meyer worked in China. He sent the first soybean to America. And persimmons! Any persimmon grown in this country today comes from that lineage. And of course, there are these lemons—named for him. Meyer died in China. He drowned in the Yangtze, pushed from a riverboat."

I looked at the trees with new appreciation.

"He sent these across the Pacific, and the Spanish sent tomatoes to Italy in the sixteenth century, and the Portuguese, chilies to India. And maybe a comet brought it all to Earth—who knows? I quite agree with Jaina Mitra."

He plucked a lemon from a tree.

"Nothing is natural."

A LONG-AWAITED ANNOUNCEMENT

THERE ARRIVED FROM HORACE a special, urgent edition of the Marrow Fair e-newsletter: there would be, the next morning, a convening of all the vendors, because Mr. Marrow intended to address his market.

Did that mean I'd finally see him?

Lily Belasco's eyes were merry when I asked. "In a manner of speaking."

"How often do *you* see him?"

She dug in the pockets of her slouchy jacket. "He's pretty hands-off, but I keep him in the loop." She produced a wide phone and waggled it. "Encrypted messages. He keeps the bank account full. What more can you ask for?"

Wandering the workstations, I heard rumors. Mr. Marrow was moving the market to Los Angeles. To Tokyo. He was shutting it down. He had run out of money. He was being pursued by the SEC. The yakuza. The Department of Health. (This last possibility seemed, to me, the most plausible.)

In the early morning, an hour before the preview was set to begin, all of us gathered in the lemon grove. Some loitered among the trees, others sat at the long picnic table. I found a seat with Orli, Naz, and Jaina Mitra. Jaina slumped, head propped up by one hand, her cheek smooshed, eyes half-lidded. She looked utterly spent.

Belasco had wheeled an enormous TV out to face the long picnic table and was now fiddling with the laptop at Naz's coffee bar, patching her phone into the sound system. The TV glared bright, basic blue, the words NO SIGNAL migrating slowly across it.

Mr. Marrow wasn't going to be here at all.

"He lives in China," Orli whispered. "It's already night-time there."

Naz looked dubious. "No, he's here with us." He lowered his voice to a hiss. "Do you see Horace anywhere? He's Horace."

"Okay, folks," Belasco called out. The depot's soundtrack went quiet and was replaced with the buzz of a phone line. At the same time, the TV showed a painted still life: a feast set up on a pockmarked table with a deep blue curtain hanging inexplicably behind it. On the table were a heel of bread and a bowl of plums. A curved knife protruded from a rump of cheese. On a bright platter there was a whole fish, its mouth frozen in an eternal yawp. Everything in the scene gleamed as if lacquered.

A voice boomed out over the speakers.

"I haven't met all of you," the voice said, "but I've tasted everything you have to offer." Its tone was deep, digitally disguised. The long space smeared it with echoes. It was as if the concourse itself were speaking to us. This was the voice of Mr. Marrow.

As for his face: with every syllable, the fish in the paint-ing moved its tiny mouth.

"I've gathered you here for a long-awaited announcement."

The juxtaposition—the booming voice, the tiny fish—was weird and hilarious. I looked around. No one was smiling.

"We've been here for a little over a year. Lily Belasco opened the doors and wheeled in the lemon trees. Some of you joined shortly after. Others have only been here a few weeks. We've been running previews all summer, and I know most of you are wondering: When do we open to the public?"

Murmurs of assent. I'd been more than busy enough serving the customers who showed up for the previews, but others were apparently ready to reach a larger market.

"There is a great realignment coming," the fish intoned. "It will be equal to the upheaval of the 1950s. You have heard me say this before. In those years, the entire experience of eating in America was remade. Packaging, refrigeration, the interstate highways—you can trace it all back. These systems were invented by particular people, at particular times, in particular places." The fish paused. "Times like now." Its glittering eyes scanned back and forth. "Places like this." Another pause. "We can build a new system."

The shiver of pleasure that ran through the assembled vendors was so intense I felt it like a rattling gust. They believed the fish. The fish was their prophet.

"On both sides, they've failed us," the fish said. "Of course, we know about the industrialists. Their corn syrup and cheese product. Their factory farms ringed by rivers of blood and shit, blazing bonfires of disease barely contained by antibiotic blankets. These are among the most disgusting scenes in the history of this planet."

Murmurs of agreement and apprehension at that.

"But on the other side . . . the organic farms, the precious restaurants . . . these are toy supply chains. 'Farm to table,' they say. Well. When you go from farm to table, you leave a lot of people out." The crowd was silent. "I think more poorly of these people than I do of the industrialists, because *they know better*. They know it's all broken, and what do they do? They plant vegetables in the backyard."

The fish would get along with Andrei.

"So that leaves *us*."

Wait, *was* the fish . . . ?

"The doors of the Marrow Fair open to the public not this Wednesday but the next."

The vendors exploded with agitation and excitement.

"That's too soon!" someone cried.

"Is there a plan for parking?" asked someone else. "I think we need a plan for parking."

The fish closed its mouth, lidded its eyes, and the painting was still. The TV went blue again, and after a moment, Naz's soundtrack resumed.

There were whoops and groans, smiles and nods, high fives that snagged the branches of the lemon trees.

Across the picnic table, Jaina Mitra looked stricken.

To no one in particular, she said, "I'm not ready yet."

QUITTING

THE MARROW FAIR was happening for real, and soon my two jobs would not coexist so comfortably. Lily Belasco expected the market's foot traffic to equal the Ferry Building's, eventually. That meant thousands of people a day. It was time to choose.

I visited General Dexterity's website. The Vitruvian 3 was calmly listed for sale at forty thousand dollars, or forty-eight with a two-year support package.

My salary was hefty, but my Cabrillo Street rent was commensurate. However, I spent basically nothing on food, transportation, health care, or entertainment, so after a year in San Francisco, my savings account had swollen to a little over ten thousand dollars.

Employment at General Dexterity carried with it a small allotment of stock options, and of those, a quarter had vested and were officially mine. The company was still privately held, almost entirely by Andrei, so I couldn't sell them directly, but there was a standing offer to impatient Dextrous from a Qatari prince who would buy our options at a slight discount. (When I first heard about this, it seemed breathtakingly exotic, possibly illegal, but the cold-eyed wraiths all shrugged. Apparently every tech company had a prince waiting in the wings.) I cashed out my options, which brought my total to thirty-seven thousand dollars.

I almost had enough to buy the Vitruvian outright, but mindful of the need to also eat and pay rent, I decided to seek additional financing.

I explained it first to Lily Belasco. "Just like he bought Jaina's sequencer," I said. "And her subscription to the microbe thing."

"How much are we talking about?"

I told her, and Belasco nodded slowly. "I'll check."

Later, she appeared at my workstation. She watched the Vitruvian work for a moment. "Forty thousand dollars, really?"

"The cost is mainly in the pressure sensors," I said. "They have twenty-four bit resolution, and the sample rate . . . Anyway, they're expensive."

Belasco initiated a call, switched her phone to speaker mode, and placed it on the ping-pong table. In another moment, the modulated voice of Mr. Marrow squawked through the little speakers. He wasted no time with a preamble.

"The problem, as I see it, is that you've done the crucial work—here in my market, I should add—as an employee of another company. Your employer owns that work, correct? So what does my investment get me?"

"I'm quitting General Dexterity." It was the first time I'd said it out loud. I felt as renegade as Beo with his restaurant. "There's so much more to do. So many skills! Knives, food processors, frying pans . . . the arm could reach right into the oil. There's a marketplace for ArmOS extensions, and I'm going to sell kitchen skills."

Mr. Marrow was silent. Then I heard a modulated sound that might have been a laugh. I looked at Belasco and mouthed, *Is he laughing?*

Mr. Marrow composed himself. "I don't understand half of what you said, which makes me think you might be onto something. Keep your savings. I'll buy the robot in exchange for twenty percent of . . . whatever this is going to be." The modulated voice was silent a moment. "Are you sure this is what you want?"

I was sure.

"Belasco, cut the check. Lois—make it work."

The phone went silent. Until that moment, I hadn't realized how much I cared about the opinion of an anonymous benefactor who sometimes inhabited the body of a painted fish. But I did.

At General Dexterity, Peter did not seem very surprised.

"We'll miss you on Control," he said, "and I know the guys at the Slurry table will miss you, too. Have you tried the latest formulation? Revision G mark . . . five, I guess? The glycemic index is unreal."

I ducked into the cafeteria to reassure Chef Kate that I would keep her supplied with sourdough even though I was leaving the company. In the kitchen, I found her robot arm wheeled out of the corner, reactivated, cracking eggs merrily alongside her sous chefs.

"I heard we have you to thank for this," Kate said drily. Her expression was complicated.

"I can't tell if you're happy about it or not," I said.

She sighed. "Neither can I."

As I was shepherded around the office, enduring various last-day-of-work rituals, I was accosted first by Arjun and then by Garrett.

"There's something you need to know," Arjun hissed as I was walking out of the HR debrief.

"There's something you need to know," Garrett whispered as I was preparing for the Proprioception handoff.

"Garrett's in love with you."

"Arjun's in love with you."

I told them both I didn't have time for this bullshit, and if anybody wanted to ask a lady out, he could do it via text message like a normal person.

Across Townsend Street, I walked the length of the Task Acquisition Center, headed for the desk of Deborah Palmer-Grill, where I would make my arrangements to purchase the refurbished arm. I peered across the rows and tried to spot the bearded chef, but of course, he was gone. I'd made him obsolete. Confidence.

DPG rose to meet me. "You did it." She reached for my hand, giving it not a mere shake but a hearty rattle. She was grinning. "I think I'm going to get a raise because of you. Andrei was obsessed with the eggs!"

I bent across her desk to reach her keyboard and tap my payment information into a digital form.

"Are you sure you don't want to stay?" DPG said. The purchase order floated on her monitor. "You could join me over on this side of Townsend Street. We would make a good team!"

I looked back at the arms and their trainers. There were fewer than before. It wasn't just the bearded chef who was gone. General Dexterity was making progress.

I shook my head. "I think I want to get a little labor in while there's still a chance."

I walked out of the robot factory into bright sunlight with my belongings in a small box. My tablet and stylus; my picture of my parents; Kubrick the cactus. It was the middle of the day and I'd deployed no office chaff. Odd parts of me, my chin and my heels and the soft backs of my arms, felt tingling and buoyant. I was light.

THE NOVICE'S GRACE

A NOTHER WEDNESDAY CAME, and with it the final market preview. Soon, our secret kingdom would open to the world. Every customer whom I'd ever seen was here this morning, snapping photos to post on the expedient image-based social network. This was their last chance to prove to the world they had been one of the elect.

I had forwarded Chaiman's album along to Naz, and this morning he played it through the concourse. Stretched out by echoes, the songs of the Mazg were sweetly sad. Valedictory. They were perfect.

There was at least one new customer on this, the last of the Wednesdays. I recognized her. Charlotte Clingstone.

"So, here you are," she said.

A trio of acolytes clustered behind her, eyes roving the concourse warily. I recognized them, too, from the kitchen at Café Candide. They all noticed the Vitruvian at once. It was mixing placidly. They stared.

"That's quite a contraption," Clingstone said. "Is it really necessary?"

"It's helpful," I said.

She lifted a loaf from the ping-pong table, faced the smiling crust squarely through her glasses. "It looks different than I remember it."

I offered her a taste. Her contingent, too.

The acolytes chewed dutifully. Clingstone sniffed the bread, raised her eyebrows, and took a nibble. "It's very competent," she said. "Do you bake anything else? Croissants? Pizza dough?"

I did not.

"You do remind me of Jim with his mystery starter. He had the novice's grace, perpetually. It was maddening." She nibbled her sourdough sample and continued, sounding very casual. "I have a proposal for you. Leave the robot behind. Come join us at Café Candide." It took her acolytes a moment to process what they'd just heard. When they did, their eyes went wide, and they looked at me with bewilderment and horror.

Clingstone continued. "Bring the starter back to the café. You'll apprentice under Mona Rahut. You met her. There's no better teacher."

I felt the disorientation of a generous offer that in no way lines up with anything you want to do: like a promotion to senior alligator wrestler, or an all-expenses-paid trip to Gary, Indiana.

"That's very kind of you," I said, "but I have a business here. They're about to open the market. It's going to get a lot bigger."

My reply pinged off Clingstone's calm countenance without leaving a mark. She chewed the last of her sample and swallowed. "Many young people wait years to be offered an apprenticeship at Café Candide." The smoldering hatred in the acolytes' gazes indicated they had recently been those people.

"I just don't see myself working in a restaurant," I said.

Clingstone's gaze was even. "It's really quite a bit more than a restaurant."

"No," I said. "Thank you." Firmly. "I've learned a lot on my own."

She *hmm*ed, and it was almost musical. She looked from me to the Vitruvian to the starter in its crock, and back to me again. "I wonder if that's true? Some days, that bread of Jim's . . . it seemed almost to bake itself."

I was going to protest, but Clingstone turned and shepherded her acolytes back onto the yellow-tape road. "Thank you for the taste," she said. "Though I do think you should try pizza dough. A killer sourdough crust. Can your robot do that?"

More customers passed by. I was reaching into the Faustofen when I heard a voice I recognized: "Lois! Proprioception!"

It was Andrei, linked arm in arm with an older man.

"What are you doing here?"

"I was invited," he said. He started to laugh. "I didn't expect to see a Vitruvian! This is the one you bought."

"She's one of your employees?" the older man asked. He was very handsome, with an old sea captain look to him.

"Was. Gregor, this is Lois Clary. Originally from Michigan. She worked with us on the Control team for . . . fourteen months?"

Those flash cards were good.

Andrei looked down the concourse. "You quit . . . to work here?"

"This is where I solved the egg problem," I told him. "I wouldn't have been able to do it at the office. I bake bread now, and I'm going to put some things up for sale in the ArmOS marketplace."

Andrei smiled at that, but still seemed perplexed. He and his companion said farewell and continued along the yellow-tape road. I told them to sample the Lembas cakes with an open mind.

Watching them walk away, it occurred to me again: Could Andrei be Mr. Marrow? They were both so deeply impatient with the world as it was . . .

Later, Charlotte Clingstone and her acolytes passed by on their way out. The acolytes looked exhausted; worn down by novelty. Clingstone spoke to them, and while they proceeded up onto the airfield, she returned to my workstation. I was afraid she was going to try again to recruit me, but she only thwapped a book down on the ping-pong table.

"From Portacio's collection," she said.

It was *Candide.*

"I read it when I was a little younger than you, and it was a formative experience. Thus, the name of the café."

I inspected the book. It was very slender.

"I think you might enjoy it," Clingstone said.

I wondered if this market was all silly gimmicks to her, or if she'd found anything at all that she actually liked.

"Yes. The mushroom grotto is interesting, isn't it? We're going to try those hen-of-the-woods."

"Did you see the Lembas cakes?"

Charlotte Clingstone smiled and winced at the same time. "It's a very impressive project, but I fear it's a bit too far ahead of the curve for Café Candide. That woman still has things to prove. But one day? Who knows. Maybe we'll start a dinner with her little cathedrals."

<FROM: BEO>

HERE'S A STORY about how the starter came to us.
The first of the Mazg, before we were the Mazg, was a man named M., who was pressed into service as a slave. He rowed aboard a ship crossing the sea. (Which sea? The story does not specify, of course!) There was a storm; the ship capsized; and this man M. washed ashore onto a great rocky island that, even though it stood along many trade routes, was uninhabited because there was no place to grow anything, and so anyone who settled there would be dependent on others for their food, and that was a losing proposition in those times, on that sea.

M. cursed his luck. His refuge was barren. There were pools of condensation in the rock, and he sipped from these while little crabs snatched at his nose.

On the third day, starving, he considered his options, which were (1) attempt to swim elsewhere, or (2) throw himself off the great rocky island's tallest outcropping. Two kinds of suicide.

Then he discovered a cave. Its opening was the narrowest crevice, invisible from any but the closest angle. He would not have discovered it if there had not been a smell emanating from inside—very faint, but in his starved state it drew him like a lure.

Lois, you know this smell.

I will write more later.

DEFLATION

A S THE MARROW FAIR ACCELERATED toward its launch, a crisis unfolded, first slow, then fast.

To ensure I could make enough loaves to sell five or six days a week, I was testing myself, with the Vitruvian slinging dough double time and the Faustofen's burners roaring nonstop. I ordered the fancy flour in bags larger than I'd known existed. To match all that flour, to mix dough in the volume I required: I needed more starter.

It felt like a kind of surrender, but I transferred the Clement Street starter from its ceramic crock into a wide plastic tub. When I began to bake, I prepared a prodigious amount of floury paste for fuel. But in its new tub, the Clement Street starter grew slowly, almost reluctantly. I put the music of the Mazg on repeat and turned up the volume; it didn't have any effect.

Worse: the loaves that resulted were deflated. Upon reflection, it had been happening for some time, just too gradually to notice. Now there was no denying it: the loaves were not as round as before, and when I tapped them on their backs, I heard unappetizing thuds. Inside, the crumb was different:

heavy and dense. The smell was off, too: less banana, more acetone. And the faces that peered up from the crust were flat masks of resignation.

I was asking a lot of the starter, I realized. But I was treating it well; I was offering it a daily feast of the finest wheat sugars! This was a partnership, a symbiotic relationship, and the starter had a job to do. The Vitruvian and I were doing ours.

I tried to negotiate with it. "What's the matter? What do you need?"

No gurgles. No puffs. No phenomena at all. The Clement Street starter seemed . . . depressed.

Each day, the starter took twice as long to double in volume. I was accustomed to the mathematics of exponentiation working in my favor; now I worried that it had turned against me. If this trend continued, there wouldn't be enough hours in the day to get what I needed for the day's loaves. The Marrow Fair's opening was approaching.

I began to quietly freak out.

It was possible I was overthinking it. The problem might be mundane. A search of Global Gluten revealed that, yes, starters sometimes lost their mojo. The customary recommendation was to throw it out and start over, but I couldn't do that. I wanted to bang on the keyboard: *WHAT IF YOUR STARTER WAS GIVEN TO YOU BY MYSTERIOUS SIBLINGS FROM AN UNKNOWN COUNTRY AND WHAT IF IT'S IRREPLACEABLE??*

Naz at the coffee bar noticed my mood. "This might be more than a cappuccino can fix," he said. I ordered one anyway, and while he was preparing it, I explained that my sourdough starter was exhibiting a pathology I couldn't diagnose.

Naz nodded sagely. "This thing"—he clonked his espresso machine on the head—"is fantastic, but it's totally temperamental. I always struggle with it. You know who turned out to be the Marzocco whisperer? Anita, with the crickets. She rebuilds old motorcycles." He clacked a cup down into its saucer and slid it across the countertop. "This place is a magnet for weirdo geniuses. Somebody at the Marrow Fair can help you. Just put a note in the newsletter."

I composed my query, stared at it on my laptop's screen for ten minutes, then sent it to Horace for inclusion in the next day's dispatch.

In the morning, Jaina Mitra found me at my workstation. I was sitting in the folding chair, waiting for a batch of dough to very slowly rise.

For once, her hair was down. It was impossibly thick—definitively a different substance than what was attached to my scalp. She was wearing a T-shirt, not her usual lab coat, and she seemed more relaxed than I'd ever seen her before. Maybe things were going well with Lembas.

"I saw your note in the newsletter," Jaina Mitra said lightly, "and . . . I have an idea. I could run your starter through the sequencer. Find out what's in there."

I got the sense she was just looking for reasons to use her amazing machine. I thought about the sequencing process as she had described it—the pulverization of the cells, the divination of their entrails. What good would it do me to know about the starter's dead DNA? It was its living behavior I needed to understand.

"I'll think about it," I said. "It's nice of you to offer. Thanks."

"Of course. Tell me what you decide. And you should come

over and try the new batch sometime. It's better! I think it's better. I'm almost there."

Nothing was happening at my workstation. The dough was going to take a very, very, very long time.

I rose from the folding chair. "Can I try it now?"

Over at Jaina Mitra's lab, I bit into one of the new Lembas cakes. The gluiness had improved, but there was a new flavor—deeply metallic. It tasted uncomfortably like blood. I winced, and I could see the disappointment in her eyes. She took a bite herself, and cursed. "Something changed. It wasn't like this last night . . ."

"It's really hard, what you're trying to do," I said. "You're inventing something totally new. Everyone else here, we're taking things that are established and . . . putting a twist on them. Even *then*, it's impossible. Trust me."

Jaina Mitra nodded absently. "I think maybe the problem is the molybdoenzymes . . ."

I walked to Naz's coffee bar and requested a glass of water to wash the coppery flavor out of my mouth, then sat at the long picnic table to check my email. Replies to my query in the newsletter were accumulating, and in their recommendations they were unanimous. Unequivocal.

Talk to Stephen Agrippa, they said.

Ask Agrippa.

Agrippa the cheese maker.

Agrippa knows more about microbes than anyone.

Agrippa, up on the airfield.

Agrippa, with the goats.

<FROM: BEO>

SO, WHAT NEXT? M. wormed his way through the narrow crevice and found a scene from a dream. Inside, the cave was forested with fungus, their stalks as thick around as trees, with fluttering ribs and wobbling tendrils. The wind across the crevice played a whistling song. (Remember this.)

M. knew that mushrooms could be deadly, but what choice did he have? He feasted. And guess what? They were great! The fruits of the cave sustained him.

Weeks later, a sharp-nosed ship ventured close enough to the great rocky island for him to signal, waving his arms atop the precipice from which he might before have jumped. When the ship approached, he climbed aboard and . . . was immediately pressed into service, a slave once more. He told no one of the cave and its hidden sustenance.

Five years later, he had earned his freedom, and five years after that, he had acquired a ship of his own, slow and leaky, but large enough to carry not only his own small family but also the families of the men beside whom he had rowed and suffered.

This part of the story feels true to me.

AGRIPPA

BEYOND THE OLD HANGARS there was the expanse of abandoned airfield, cracked and overtaken by tall grasses. A line of low, rounded bunkers rose at the asphalt's edge, and beyond them it was just dark water.

I carried a sample of the Clement Street starter in its original ceramic crock across the broken landscape, the Marrow Fair beneath my feet.

The man and his alpaca were out there guarding their herd.

I approached slowly, both of them watching me as I crossed the concrete.

"Stephen Agrippa?" I called when I was close enough. "We met before . . . never mind. I work in the market." I pointed dumbly into the ground. "Everyone said I should talk to you."

The man nodded slowly at this.

"I have something strange," I said. "It's a sourdough starter, but it's not— Hey!"

A goat was gnawing on my pant leg. I danced away. Agrippa laughed; a high, echoing bark.

"Come on," he said. "Bring your something strange. Don't worry about Hercules. He's cool." His voice was wry and reedy. He turned and ambled away. I followed, circling wide around the hungry goat and the watchful alpaca, whose name was apparently Hercules.

Agrippa led me toward one of the bunkers, set deep into the ground, its rounded top thick with vegetation, inky green and rusty red. The bunker's face was a half-moon of white. There was a ramshackle Airstream set up next to it with an awning that extended to one side.

In the shade of the awning, Agrippa reached into a plastic cooler and retrieved two bottles, both unlabeled. He cracked their caps with his molars. "Want one?"

I accepted my beer from the master of microbes and spun the blank bottle. "Home brew?"

"It's from Algebra, around the way." He motioned back toward the brewery. "Quintuple-hopped. Experimental. I help 'em out sometimes."

"People say you're a microbe whisperer."

He took a swig from his bottle, looked out across the water. "They do say that. I try to discourage them, but then they ask me what I *am*, and I can never quite say it right. So then I just shut up."

"You make cheese."

He made a deep *Mm-hmm*, jerked a thumb at the bunker behind him. "That's the cheese cave. Used to hold nukes." He took another swig of beer. Grinned. "And now it holds some *truly* advanced technology."

A nervous itch spread across my scalp. "Is it safe to be here?"

"Do you drive here in a car?"

"I take Carl's ferry."

"Well, it's safer than that."

"I mean, is it radioactive?"

"Everything's radioactive. It's fine. Mutation's a good thing."

I had no idea if he was serious or not. He seemed like the kind of person who cultivated that ambiguity—who reveled in it.

Generally I don't enjoy those kinds of people.

I hefted the Clement Street starter in its crock and held it out to Agrippa for inspection. He eyed it, then me.

"Oh, I can't do anything about that."

"What?"

"You think I'm a sourdough mechanic, and you just drop it off? No, ma'am. I will tell you what I know. How you apply that knowledge to *your* particular technology there is up to you."

"You keep calling it technology."

"Technology it is. Come on. I want you to see the cave."

INSIDE THE BUNKER, the air was clammy and dense, heavy with a ripe ammoniac smell. It seemed to crawl up inside my nose and elbow other odors away. The bunker was narrow but deep—deep enough, at least, that the light from the open door did not illuminate the back wall and instead only petered out into darkness.

Wire shelves ran straight down the long space, like an art school demonstration of perspective and foreshortening. The shelves were laden with huge wheels of cheese that I recognized from Orli's table at the Marrow Fair. They were veined with bright colors: blue and turquoise, flame orange, hot pink.

Agrippa carried a basket under his arm as he walked slowly through the bunker, scanning up and down like a value-conscious shopper scouring the shelves at a grocery store.

"If you sit here in the dark," he said absently—and it was no stretch to imagine him doing so—"and wait a long time . . . you see yellow flashes. That's vitamin B$_2$ fluorescing."

"And you are one hundred percent sure it's not dangerous."

"It's beautiful."

That was not a satisfying response.

We passed a shelf where a wheel of cheese had exploded into some kind of fungal overgrowth. Tall, mushroom-like fruiting bodies rose up and swayed slightly in the air disturbed by our passage. I sucked in a sharp breath.

"Is that . . . there . . ." I pointed. "Is that all right?"

Agrippa nodded. "Oh, it's fantastic. An empire is rising, lifting up great works."

He picked up a wheel on the next shelf, held it close to his nose. Then he fished a tool out of his pocket, some kind of metal syringe, and plunged it into the wheel. He extracted a slender core sample, popped part of it into his mouth. Offered me the other part. I hesitated for a moment, then accepted it. Satisfied, he turned around and headed for the exit.

"*Culture*," he said. "The word meant *this*—making cheese—before it meant *that*—art and opera. And before it meant anything, it just meant working the land. That's a better definition. That's who we are. Not our music, our books. *Psh*, books. They're all dead. We're alive. We eat, we grow. But, but but but, here's the thing! We're amateurs."

We emerged back onto the airfield. I was happy to be out of the bunker.

"Amateurs!" Agrippa repeated. "Compared to what you just saw? This is the key to my cheese, to that beer, to your sourdough, to anything and everything. I'm going to say it, and you're going to nod like you get it, but you won't. Not yet. It doesn't come easy."

He took a breath.

"In that cave, empires are rising and falling. There are battles under way. Wars. More soldiers on both sides than in all the wars of human history combined. And they are *struggling*. They are taking territory, making it safe. Building fortresses." He lifted the wheel he'd chosen out of his basket and hefted it. "There is a saga in here to put our whole history to *shame*."

His eyes were a little defocused now, lost in the grandeur of his rant.

"In every wheel of cheese, there's revolution, alliance, betrayal . . . Can you feel it?"

I told him the truth: I could not.

"Nope. You're honest, I appreciate that. Of course you can't. I couldn't, not at first. We're blind to it. But this is their world, not ours, and their stories are greater."

I frowned. "They're just bacteria. They don't think or plan. They just . . . exist."

"Just *exist*? They do things we only dream of. They are fecund and potent, they can speak to one another with chemicals and light, they can form teams—oh, the teams they can form. Millions strong, all working together perfectly. If we could cooperate like that—if we could even get close—we would have all of our problems solved. They can live at the bottom of the ocean. They can live in volcanoes. They can live forever."

Well: my comrades below had sent me to the right person. This was a man who loved microbes.

He looked at me, eyes blazing. "This is all I have to offer you. If you can understand this—if you can not only hear what I'm saying but *believe* it—then you'll know what to do with your starter."

We were both silent a moment. Then I ventured: "Can you at least give me a hint?"

He laughed. "Sure. What I'm saying is, first you have to respect it."

He spun his wheel of cheese around and sniffed it, sucking in a great deep breath. Then he held it out, turned it a degree either way, inspecting, and the look on his face showed more than respect. It showed awe.

O N THE GREAT ROCKY ISLAND, M. built a kingdom! His friends and family feasted on the fruits of the cave and they were well nourished. They built a long jetty, a place where ships could pause on their journeys across the sea. To feed the sailors, the Mazg brewed beer and baked bread. The fluttering, wobbling culture of the cave, they kept secret.

This is a pretty good story so far, but maybe you're wondering, Why haven't I heard of M.'s great rocky island? Why is it not a wealthy maritime state? Why are Beo and his cousins hidden away in all the second-story apartments of Europe?

Because, of course, there was a problem.

Their port was very successful, and the population of the Mazg (we can call them that now) grew rapidly in just a few generations. They became beer-drinkers and bread-eaters themselves, because the culture of the cave thrived nowhere else, not even in other caves on the island. For a long time, they wondered why. Most shrugged. Then a girl of the Mazg, a genius, simply opened her ears. The whistling song across the narrow crevice was linked somehow to the life of the culture. Through experimentation, she determined the crucial tones and sequences. This is the origin of the songs that the Mazg sing today—the songs on your CD.

This girl became the governor of the great rocky island, and she transformed it, bringing the culture out of the cave. Now the Mazg had beer and bread and something else, too. Sailors who tied up their ships and walked ashore to rest and trade were well fed and well treated, but they were not allowed behind the walls of the fortresses in which the culture of the Mazg was propagated and the songs of the Mazg were sung.

Behind those walls, the language of the Mazg grew in upon itself and lost its kinship with other languages.

AGRIPPA (CONTINUED)

IRETURNED TO THE AIRFIELD the next day because the others had spoken the truth: Agrippa was a genius. Maybe also an asshole. But I believed he had something to teach me; I believed he understood the starter in a way I didn't, or couldn't.

The cheese is not the thing, he told me. The cheese is just the territory, the battleground. The bacteria are the thing. They are the actors on a milky stage.

Most plants have at least one bacterial symbiote, he told me. He pronounced it carefully: *sym-bi-ote*. He looked out across the airfield, at the scrubby red and green plants. All those? Infected. But that's not the right word, he said. Infected means there's something wrong. This is all right; it's partnership. Some plants are infected by bacteria that are themselves infected by a virus. Wheels within wheels. Clockwork.

You have four pounds of bacteria in your body, he said. You don't feel it. He bounced on his heels. I think I'm starting to feel it. I think I can talk to them.

Talk to them?

Yes, he said. Send them messages. Chemicals. Hormones. What I want to do next is learn how to listen and hear their reply.

He held one of the wheels of cheese under my nose and instructed me to breathe deeply. I did. The smell was dense and close, but there was also the suggestion of citrus—a far-off orange.

What would it be like, he asked, to smell our whole world at once? Our whole history? If this wheel were *us*, what would it smell like? Agrippa thought it would smell like engine exhaust.

He seemed barely to eat, and the things he did eat were strange: extremely funky yogurt, strained and thickened, along with tiny wild radishes foraged in the far corners of the airfield.

Once, I asked him: Do you . . . shower? He shrugged and said: The last time I showered was before I arrived here. Almost a year ago.

A year without a shower! The idea of it made my skin crawl. And he did have a ripeness to him, but like the cheese he created, it wasn't unpleasant. Agrippa had achieved equilibrium. He had won the inhabitants of his underarms to his cause.

One day, Agrippa said: I dream of a great council of fermentation. Beer. Sauerkraut. Kimchi! Have you had kimchi? I love kimchi.

My phone reception was terrible on the airfield. It was an uncanny spot: really truly in the center of everything—with San Francisco's skyline visible across the water, the great bustle of the Port of Oakland across the channel, Oakland's own downtown rising in the other direction, the Marrow Fair beneath us—yet it felt utterly desolate and disconnected. It was amazing to see the goats grazing here in the calm eye of a storm of trade and transit.

I came to visit again the next day, and the next. Mainly, I listened to Agrippa talk. When he didn't talk, I followed him around, enjoying the silence. I followed him into the bunker, tried to see what he saw in the developing wheels of cheese. Mostly, I failed. I tried to be helpful. He would show me how to do something, and I would do it.

I milked a goat.

I learned how he made his cheese. He painted it. Literally: He painted bacteria and fungi onto the wheel. Dipped a brush into a scummy pool of some culture, dragged long wet strokes across the curd's pale surface. In the cave, after weeks of development, these strokes took on texture and color, became deep blue or hot pink or flame orange, or even exhibited a ghostly bioluminescence.

I had my first tiny breakthrough when I looked at one of his painted wheels and saw not a lump of milk by-product inoculated with bacteria, but a *map*, color-coded just like an atlas. For a moment, I saw the battle lines. There were mighty armies on the march, billions strong or more, deploying biochemical matériel, fighting a war that was going to take, on their timescale, millennia or more, maybe millions of years, because it was for them an evolutionary timescale. They could change. The organisms that won the war might not be the organisms that began it. For a moment, I saw it. Blue and pink and orange.

I found Agrippa farther back in the bunker.

"I saw it," I told him. That's all.

He looked at me—his face changed, eyes narrowed, then

opened again—and he nodded once. "Good. Now you know what to do with your starter."

Did I?

I sat with the ceramic crock in the deck chair next to the Airstream. It was nighttime, past ten. The sun was down, but the Port of Oakland lit the airfield with a purgatorial glow. I wondered how the goats handled the strange light. They must have adapted.

Agrippa and I were sipping experimental beers. I was a little bit drunk.

"I think . . . my starter needs a warrior spirit," I said.

"It *has* a warrior spirit," he said. "It was born with it."

"Then what's the problem?"

"You need to give it something to fight."

"Like what?"

"A rival. Another culture. Something from Big Sourdough." He paused. "Is there such a thing as Big Sourdough?"

I considered the question. The answer came to me.

"I can use King Arthur," I declared.

"That's flour, right?"

"Yes, but, but but but"—I was getting excited—"they also sell a starter, they say it's a hundred years old . . . They ship it to you. It's really popular. They must make it by the barrel."

"Ohhhh," he said. "Perfect. Get some of that. Put them in the arena together."

"What if the King Arthur wins?"

"Hey now! You gotta believe in your starter," he said. "It can hear you. It's right there. *You* need to have a warrior spirit, too! Lead the way!"

I stood up. Stared down into the crock. The pale gray

scum was no less pale, gray, or scummy than ever before. "Are you ready to fight?" I asked it.

"There you go," Agrippa said.

"Are you ready to fight?" I cried.

"There you go!"

"Are you ready to fight?!"

I held the crock over my head and stomped my feet. A starburst of shadows spun around me, cast by the lights of the bridge and the port and the city and the brewery, all the lights of civilization.

Agrippa got up, too, and started howling and dancing along. The goats stayed on the far side of the airfield—wisely— but Hercules the alpaca wandered closer, curious.

WHAT NEXT? Beyond the great rocky island, the world was shifting, and now the richest trade routes crossed other seas. Fewer ships stopped at the jetty; fewer sailors bought beer and bread. But the Mazg were still full of ambition! They had hardly begun their story. They used their accumulated wealth to acquire ships of their own, and armed themselves, and became pirates.

For a while, this was extremely successful. When Mazg pirates stormed a ship, they had the advantage, always, for while the other crew was sick from moldy rations, the pirates were strong from rations made of mold. The great rocky island was now a single enormous fortress-pantry, teeming with the fluttering, wobbling culture that sustained the Mazg. They sang their songs louder. They sang them faster. They were hungry. They were unstoppable!

They didn't realize the danger they were in. Something important had been lost. In case it's not obvious—it's easier to communicate this when you tell the story out loud, like my uncle does—this story wants you to think that maybe that something was humility.

After a long season of piracy, one of the roving ships of the Mazg returned to the great rocky island only to find that the great rocky island was gone. In its place there was a floating forest of fungus with fluttering ribs and wobbling tendrils, many times larger than the great rocky island had ever been. While they watched in horror, it fluttered and wobbled and . . . burped.

Lost was the kingdom of the Mazg—eaten, in the end, by its own food.

That last ship fled to land. The Mazg aboard carried in their crocks the culture of the cave, and in their memories the songs. Everything else was lost.

It's just a story. There's another one, about a girl named Mazga who steals the culture from the queen of the dead. In that story, the songs are the memories of sad souls, and they are needed to trick the culture into believing it's still in the underworld. Shehrieh likes that one better.

Me, I like the pirates.

THE FALL OF CAMELOT

THE KING ARTHUR FLOUR COMPANY began as a Boston-based importer in 1790 and introduced its own American-grown wheat flour in 1896. Since 2004, it's been one hundred percent employee-owned, which is pretty cool. The company's headquarters, now located in Vermont, is an enormous twelve-sided building called Camelot.

From Camelot's website, I ordered the King Arthur sourdough starter (a single ounce) and paid extra for expedited shipping. The UPS driver delivered it to Cabrillo Street in a plain brown box. Inside, there was a very small plastic tub with a white screw-on lid.

I carried the King Arthur starter to Alameda, transferred it into a larger container, and began to feed it on the same schedule as the Clement Street starter. It grew eagerly, bubbling and expanding. Where the Clement Street starter smelled faintly of bananas, the King Arthur smelled strongly of flour, with maybe a touch of vinegar. I got the sense that's how sourdough starter was supposed to smell. Its surface was wet and gloppy; there was no suggestion of the silvery tautness that was the signature of the Clement Street starter's occasional sentience.

I tried to see it through Agrippa's eyes—imagined the King Arthur starter a civilization on the rise. Was it bland, a bit boring? Maybe, but so was my own human civilization. I imagined myself as a cell down there among the teeming trillions. Maybe I was happy. Maybe I was excited for the future.

Then I carried the King Arthur starter across my workstation to meet its neighbor. It was time for an apocalypse.

I portioned off a section of the Clement Street starter, noting its despondence, and dropped it into a fresh tub—a great arena—then added the King Arthur and swirled them together. The mixture turned an even gray. For just a moment, I wondered if I had made a miscalculation, and if the King Arthur, with its Protestant work ethic, might be the stronger substance.

I whispered encouragements to the home team. "You're Alexander the Great. Rising China. Everybody better get out of your way."

The starters spasmed in slow motion. The tub frothed with gas, emitted gouts of scent new and strange: not only bananas and flour but also orange peel, Earl Grey, gunpowder. Was I detecting signal flares launched above a vast battlefield? Or was it the wreckage of war—the broken remnants of armies cleaved apart? Was I smelling corpses?

It took an hour. By the end of it, the scent of flour was gone, and the Clement Street starter was frothing, victorious. I hadn't seen it so lively since the early days, before the Marrow Fair, before anything.

I added this rampant culture to a tub with flour and water and salt and I mixed the dough myself. It bucked and surged; it was uncanny. I formed a loaf and nothing stuck to my fingers. Silvery and taut, this was sourdough on a wartime footing.

The finished loaf emerged from the Faustofen perfectly round and buoyant. Its face bore a new expression: an even, distant look, hollow-eyed like a statue from antiquity. It was a face full of grim purpose. When I tapped it on its back, I heard an echoing boom.

Lois! I haven't heard from you in a while. How is your robot doing? How's the starter?

TEND YOUR GARDEN

THE CLEMENT STREET STARTER had changed, perhaps irrevocably. Before, I sustained it with inert flour. Now it would accept only living fuel, and only in large quantities.

Every morning was a new conquest. The starter was jubilant, and I was back on track, production-wise. I had the volume of starter I needed, which meant I could mix the amount of dough I required, which meant I could bake enough bread to supply Chef Kate every day and, with luck, meet the demand that was imminent.

But as the mornings passed, I grew uneasy. The floury scent of the King Arthur starter was so innocent. When I scooped up the little utopia and dropped it into the arena with the Clement Street starter, I felt a twinge of . . . something. More than a twinge. It was as if trillions of voices suddenly cried out in terror . . .

Agrippa's logic had led me to this strategy, and to the survival of the Clement Street starter. But Agrippa's logic also demanded that I see it this way: not as a simple kitchen operation, but as a clash of civilizations.

It seemed silly to attach such a grandiose label to something so small . . . but was it really small? There had to be a scale somewhere—the scale of stars, the scale of far-off cosmic super-beings—upon which we ourselves, we humans with our cities and bridges and subterranean markets, would look like the lactobacilli and the yeast.

To them, I was the cosmic super-being, and what did I wreak with my vast and implacable powers? Total war. Utter annihilation.

I oscillated between finding this vision totally ridiculous and finding it deadly serious.

The bread had never been better! The faces in the crust were stoic and satisfied. Some of the scent of domination lingered in the finished loaves. Lily Belasco noticed the difference. "It's a bit . . . peaty," she said. "How do you do that?"

What I thought was: *Well, every morning, I sacrifice a teeming civilization to the Clement Street war machine.*

What I said was: "Who knows! Ha-ha! Sourdough is complicated!"

Agrippa had solved my problem, and he had created a new one.

I'd known the Clement Street starter wasn't normal, of course, but I honestly hadn't realized the depth of its strangeness until now, because the King Arthur starter was *very* normal. It was happy and dopey like a big brown dog. It had no special high-maintenance desires. It just wanted to grow.

I let it.

Every day, the Clement Street starter required a larger sacrifice. It was absurd: I was brewing the King Arthur starter in garbage bins. Now, instead of adding the King Arthur to the Clement Street, I did the reverse. Only the tiniest trace of the culture of the Mazg was required. I tipped a cup over and deployed a dollop of hunter/killer starter, potent and relentless. In just fifteen minutes it would sweep through the whole bin, destroying/consuming/reproducing, venting plumes of banana and gunpowder. When it was finished, nothing of the happy floury folk remained.

AS I WAS DOING THIS, I was also reading the book that Charlotte Clingstone had selected from Horace's library and left for me, *Candide*—her café's namesake.

It was, unexpectedly, a screwball action comedy. The hapless main character, whose name was Candide, traveled with a band of companions from Europe to the New World and back. Along the way, characters were flogged, shipwrecked, enslaved, and nearly executed several times. There were earthquakes and tsunamis and missing body parts.

One of Candide's companions, Pangloss, whose name I recognized from the hundred-dollar adjective he inspired—I'd never known the etymology—insisted throughout that all their misfortunes were for the best, for they delivered the companions into situations that seemed, at first, pretty good. Until those situations, too, went to shit.

The story concluded on a small farm outside Istanbul, where Candide plunked a hoe into the dirt and declared his intention to retreat from adventure (and suffering) and simply tend his garden.

The way the author told it—the book was written in 1759—it was clear I was supposed to think Candide had finally discovered something important.

I could see why the book appealed to Charlotte Clingstone. It was a rejection of ambition; a blueprint for her small, perfect, human-scale restaurant—a safe space set apart from the scrum of the world.

NOW THAT THE CLEMENT STREET STARTER was back on track, even if distressingly, I had to contend with my other limitations. The Vitruvian was working as fast as possible, but not fast enough. I needed another arm, but that wasn't in the budget. Not yet.

So I joined it.

We stood side by side. I watched it work, every so often adjusting my motions to match its hyperefficiency. The student became the master.

Other vendors, in the days before the market's public launch, had started to stay overnight. They unrolled sleeping bags in the lemon grove and slept there. I joined them.

The depot sustained me. I wolfed down cricket cookies and tube-fish tacos and Lembas cakes, which had somehow gotten even worse—now both gritty *and* gluey—but they kept me going. I drank ten coffees a day. When Naz wasn't around, I operated the espresso machine myself, and my drinks were quadruple shots.

I was working more hours than I ever had at General Dexterity, but here, I was ecstatic. I hardly worried about anything; for days I would enter states of perfect flow, eating/drinking/feeding/folding/baking/sleeping. While I slept, the Vitruvian still worked.

Then, one morning, I overslept beneath the lemon trees. I

must have looked mildly postapocalyptic as I sprinted up the concourse: hair wild, eyes dimmed, clothes stale with bits of cricket cookie on them.

When I reached my workstation, I discovered the tub that contained the Clement Street starter tipped onto its side, and a taut, silvery tendril extending outward, reaching for the King Arthur where it waited in its garbage bin. The tendril flexed and flowed. The Vitruvian had retracted and was watching it warily. It wasn't programmed to handle this.

The sight jolted me out of whatever dream I'd been lost in. This was not okay.

I had to stop. I had to figure out what I was dealing with.

I ROSE FROM MY SLEEPING BAG in the middle of the night. The depot was quiet, powered down. The only light came from the grow rooms.

I carried the Clement Street starter in front of me—now transferred back into its ceramic crock, quarantined—and padded in my socks toward Jaina Mitra's laboratory.

There, I found the hulking sequencer, the ILLUMINA HYPER CENSUS, its plastic carapace gleaming in the darkness, a line of pinprick status lights rippling silently. It seemed to be twiddling its thumbs.

I fumbled around the lab, looking for one of the sample plates. I opened one cabinet, found the Lembas cakes assembling themselves, closed it. Opened another. *There.*

Jaina Mitra had only needed a tiny bit of Horace's saliva. I dabbed my finger into the crock and let a dollop of starter ooze onto the plate. I pressed the button to open the machine, and its tray extended, along with a wash of blue light from its glowing heart. I put the sample plate into the tray and pressed the button again. It was simple; there was only one button to press. This machine that could crack the code of life was easier to operate by far than the Faustofen, or even my microwave.

The machine reclaimed the tray and began to hum.

I whispered an apology for the massacre to come. Then I sat on the floor.

Minutes passed. The hum gave way to the pulse of abrasion, then a high-pitched whine. Then silence.

I would take the information I gleaned from this machine and enter it into an expedient internet search engine. There would be something, surely, about this organism. A warning. A remedy.

I was waiting for the machine to chime, but there was no chime.

I wandered through the sleeping depot, carrying the Clement Street starter with me in its crock.

I wandered through Horace's library. Up and down the vehicle ramp. Through a loop of corridors I'd never found before, which deposited me back near the door to the tiny pier. Then I followed the corridor toward the cricket farm. I could hear them chirping.

This time, I pressed ahead.

They lived in row houses made from corrugated cardboard and superfine netting. I saw them milling around, climbing on top of one another, jumping and flickering, chittering and chirping.

What were the epic sagas of the cricket kingdom?

From back in the concourse, I heard a low and commanding chime.

HUNGER

L ATER THAT MORNING, with the first light of day peeking in through the skylight above the lemon grove, I was forming one set of loaves while the arm mixed a batch of dough when Jaina Mitra appeared, fully suited up in her lab coat again.

I curled my face into the beginning of an apology, but she held up a hand preemptively. "I'm not angry," she said. "Well, I am. You should have just accepted my offer and let me help you. But it doesn't matter."

I stood there with a cold lump of dough in my hands. "Is that all, then?"

Jaina Mitra's nostrils flared. "Not by a long shot." The slashes under her eyes seemed darker than usual. She tossed a printout onto the countertop. "I've never seen anything like it."

I recognized the spiky cascade from the screen attached to the sequencer; it was exactly what I'd seen in the middle of the night, found inscrutable, emailed to myself, and, after reviewing it in the morning, still found inscrutable. This printout was wildly annotated in bright green ink—little blobs and whorls and, above the graph, an exclamation in Jaina Mitra's blocky handwriting: *WOW!*

"Listen to what I'm saying," she said. "Sourdough starter is a community of organisms. You know that, right?"

"Yes. Of course." Everett Broom taught me that.

"Generally, there are two or three different species living together. That's what they say at the bread lab."

"There's a bread lab?"

"Washington State. They do very good work. *Maybe* four species can live together in a stable community. But this is the sequencer's report on your starter. You saw this?" I nodded, and Jaina Mitra snorted lightly. "I almost cried."

She smoothed the printout flat on the countertop and pulled a green-barreled pen from her lab coat.

"This here"—she indicated the graph's broadest peak with the pen's tip—"this is the yeast. And this"—she indicated another peak—"is *Lactobacillus sanfranciscensis*." She pronounced it carefully. "These—" She danced the tip of her pen along a series of sharper spikes. "These are matches for bacteria in the Global Microbiome Survey. It adds up to a lot more than four, obviously." Then she traced a wide box around the series of spikes that rippled along the graph's floor. "And these—there are so many of them—these are novel." She raised both eyebrows.

Apparently that did not impress me as much as it should have.

"*Meaning*," she went on, "there are no matches in the library. That, by itself, isn't so strange; like I told you, my cabinet is full of novel organisms. What's strange is finding this many taxa, known and unknown, living together in an apparently stable community." She paused. Looked at me. Over at my workstation. Back at me. "It *is* stable, isn't it?"

It felt like she was asking about me, not the starter. "I've been baking with this starter for months. I got it from a baker who had it for—years? Yes, it's stable."

She tsked. It was a tsk of awe. "There must be a hundred constituents! The smallest spikes might be noise—it's hard to tell. But even so, this many! It's a scale and complexity of commensal behavior beyond anything I've ever seen or read about." Jaina Mitra looked like she wanted to shake me. "It is *unreal.*"

WE SAT WITH OUR ESPRESSO CUPS beneath the lemon trees and I told her the starter's story. Jaina Mitra did not make a good audience; her gaze was hard and hungry, and she scrawled notes as I spoke, page after page of them in green ink. She made me nervous.

I finished by explaining the starter's decline, my consultation with Stephen Agrippa, its resurgence, and my concern that I'd taken it too far. Because I didn't understand what I was working with.

Jaina Mitra stared down at her notes. "Everyone in my field is obsessed with identifying new organisms," she murmured. "It's like a treasure hunt. But I already have the organisms I need. I just can't put them together." She looked up, staring into space. "How do their communities work? I try . . ." She sighed raggedly. "When I move one piece, the others don't fit anymore. When I turn one knob, the other knobs eat it for dinner. My new batch is worse than ever. Do you know what makes it so sticky? It's not the enzymes.

It's what the enzymes *produce*. Dead cells. Lysed bacteria. Corpses!"

The gluey taste of death. Great.

Jaina Mitra was showing me something real, and it ran a little ragged, and it made me like her a little more. Like, two percent more.

She laid her hands flat on her notebook. "I'd like to study your starter."

"I don't think it's going to solve your problem." I said it as lightly as I could.

Her face was a mask of control. "It might. Please. We could work together." She was suddenly sweet and solicitous, and it was very strange. She should have stayed sharp and brusque. She should have commanded: *Let me work with that muck of yours!* I would have complied in a moment.

THE SLURRY FACTORY

I T WAS THE DAY BEFORE the Marrow Fair's grand opening, and I was relaxing at my workstation, satisfied with my ability to produce enough sourdough, wasting time on the internet, and still thinking about Jaina Mitra's offer when she appeared again to announce she wanted to show me something that could, or should, influence my decision. It involved a car trip, and could I take the afternoon off? I accepted. I had the feeling, suddenly, that I'd been down in the darkness of the depot for too long.

A year in California and I'd rarely been south of Daly City, never stepped foot in San Jose, and barely contemplated the existence of the San Joaquin Valley.

Driving down California State Route 99 in the passenger seat of Jaina Mitra's blue Tesla, the rightmost lane was taken up completely by semis hauling trailers, and beyond them endless orchards, silvery olive trees alternating with spiky almond trees, solid green to the horizon. The San Joaquin Valley's existence was confirmed.

We watched a pickup truck with a portable toilet in its

bed crawling along an access road, keeping pace with the pickers who were sweeping across the field in a loose line.

There were structures that poked out in places: immense, featureless white warehouses, like big-box stores before any branding had been applied. We saw grain elevators, smelled feedlots.

Jaina Mitra eased onto an exit ramp and turned onto a long, straight road called Avenue 16. We passed a neon-green tractor lumbering on the shoulder and I waved to its driver, who waved back. Farther up, we watched a small plane fly in low arcs over a vast field of pistachio trees, leaving a trail of pink vapor. I fumbled with the Tesla's control panel and set the AC to recirculate.

We turned off Avenue 16 onto Road 23. There were too many long, straight roads out here to bother with names.

A semi was rattling up the road, coming in the opposite direction. The trailer it hauled was painted bright green, and as it passed, I saw a familiar logotype rendered in crisp white. That semi was hauling nutritive gel.

This was Slurry country.

The facility was ahead. It was enormous, one mile square, a tangle of towering vats with pipes and valves embroidering their surfaces, all of it bounded by loading docks where more bright green trailers were waiting. Train tracks ran straight through the facility; Slurry could be lowered in containers directly onto freight cars and hauled away to Chicago or New York or the Port of Oakland and points beyond.

Olive trees lined the long driveway that led from Road 23 into the facility. Beneath the trees, fruit rotted in dark piles.

"THIS FACILITY USED TO BELONG TO GALLO," Jaina Mitra said. "They made like ten percent of the country's wine here."

A man was crossing the parking lot to meet us. He was tall and bald and frighteningly gaunt, waving energetically, his lips pressed flat in an enthusiastic smile.

"Dr. Mitra! Yes! And our guest of honor!"

"This is Dr. Klamath," Jaina Mitra said. Her face was cheery but her eyes betrayed a sense of duty. "Founder and CEO of Slurry."

"I prefer Chief Nutrition Officer!" He gave Jaina Mitra a feather-light hug, then offered his hand to me. Taking it, I encountered a palm of extraordinary dryness.

"Come in, come in," he said. "See the sights. Dr. Mitra told me you're a Slurry subscriber—well, it all comes from here."

"I *was* a subscriber," I said. "I haven't had it in a while."

He grinned, unbowed. "It's getting better all the time!"

Inside, the air was dense and smelled slightly sour. Every surface, walls and ceiling, was braided with pipes painted primary colors, some as skinny as my wrist, others fat enough to admit Jaina Mitra's Tesla, all connecting an array of enormous vats marked with cryptic identifiers. It looked like a power plant or a refinery. In a way, it was both.

Klamath spun around and continued to speak as he led us, walking backward, toward one of the vats. This was not his first tour.

"Farmers in Fresno talk about yield per acre. That's economic, not human. So what if you're growing four tons of alfalfa per acre? Talk to me about *people*. How many people's lives are you supporting? How many *healthy* lives?"

That seemed like a reasonable question.

"Slurry is one hundred percent vertically integrated here, so I can tell you, this unit"—he patted a mammoth vat affectionately—"supports two thousand people every week. *Two thousand!*"

Two thousand students lived in my college dorm. I imagined all of them lined up in front of the vat, bowls in hand, waiting to get their daily ration of dystopia.

"We put in just five thousand dollars' worth of raw ingredients. As Dr. Mitra can tell you, it used to be a lot more. We're making it more efficient. You know what my goal is? Everybody says this is crazy, but I say it's physics. An average person uses about three kilowatt hours of energy every day. Just to live. You know the price of three kilowatt hours in California? Forty-five cents. That's our goal. It ought to be just like plugging yourself into the wall."

"That sounds pretty robotic," I said. "And I say that as someone who likes robots."

"I just want everybody to be healthy," Klamath said. His bulldozer enthusiasm faltered; I detected a note of weariness. "We should be way past this already. I want people to have time to do the things they want, rather than work to make money to buy food, or scrounge around in the kitchen."

He stopped, and steepled his fingers theatrically.

"But I know people don't want to eat gray goo. I do. That's why Dr. Mitra's work is so important. That's why we want to acquire Lembas."

Ah. It came into focus.

Klamath was leading us through the vats, toward the farthest corner of the facility.

"Those fields you drove through? That whole system? It's a dead end."

It seemed like a rather large and vibrant dead end.

"Here, we can program a yeast to make anything. Gasoline. Heroin."

Hummus?

"Not yet. But damn it, we are *close*. Dr. Mitra's work is the key. Right now, I can get one organism going . . . a yeast, or a bacteria like *E. coli*. But we want more complex products. We need to assemble and train whole communities."

Like Lembas.

"Like your starter," Jaina Mitra said lightly.

Listening to Dr. Klamath talk, hearing him slam the old system, seeing the resources he commanded, it struck me: Was I speaking to Mr. Marrow?

THE VAT WAS THE SAME SHAPE as the one in Jaina Mitra's lab, but ten times as large, a monstrous egg of shining stainless steel. A neat sign on the front read COMMUNITY PRODUCTION TEST, which sounded sort of nice. Healthy.

Klamath patted the vat affectionately. "It's cute, right? We run our wacky experiments in these little ones. I want to give it to Dr. Mitra. And this, too." He stepped over to a plastic-clad box the size of a mini-fridge—another flawlessly anonymous piece of biotech gear. "This is brand-new, which is why it looks like shit. It can build microorganisms from scratch. We hollow out a yeast, squirt in some new DNA, boot it up."

I frowned. "You just hollow . . . out . . ."

Dr. Klamath gave the box a quick caress, let his hand linger. "It's a printer for life."

Jaina Mitra extended a finger to touch it, too. Their affection for this anonymous machine was palpable. "These are impossible to get."

I looked up and considered the vat. It was bigger than my apartment.

"You can't just feed my starter flour and water," I said. "Not if you want to make this much. It likes King Arthur." I paused. "You can get it online."

"Or we could try feeding it Slurry," Jaina Mitra said, and Dr. Klamath nodded gamely. Would the Clement Street starter eat Slurry? Possibly. Would its farts be as fragrant as mine had been? Probably.

Dr. Klamath squared himself to me. "Here's the thing. Before I give Dr. Mitra the go-ahead to get this revved up, we need some legal protection. No big deal, just something that says you give us the right to exploit this biological IP that you control, et cetera, et cetera. I've got the contracts ready. I want to make it worth your while, and give you a stake in the outcome of this project. If you have questions, that's why we're here. I hope you find this as exciting as we do."

Jaina Mitra's face grew solemn. "My deal with Mr. Marrow was that he got twenty percent of Lembas. If this is as big as Dr. Klamath thinks it can be . . . that could mean millions of dollars for the Marrow Fair."

Hearing that sum, Dr. Klamath made a face as if he'd just eaten something bad. "We're not playing for pocket change here. We're playing for the whole future of food."

But was this deal exclusive?

Dr. Klamath rolled his eyes. "What? No. Keep baking.

It's great. I mean, I don't eat bread, but Dr. Mitra says it's great."

Walking back toward the lobby, I considered the vastness of the facility. If Jaina Mitra's work was successful—if she used whatever talent was hidden in the Clement Street starter to stabilize and support Lembas, to make it viable—it was possible that all of these vats might be turned over to its production.

This was scale.

It was two thousand people sustained by a single vat.

For the Clement Street starter, it would be a conquest unimaginable.

ON THE RIDE HOME, Jaina Mitra explained that if I agreed to license the Clement Street starter to her, I would receive fifty thousand shares, or five percent, of Lembas Labs, an LLC set to be acquired, soon, by Slurry Systems of Fresno, California.

"Those shares could be worth a lot of money," she said.

There was my nineteen million dollars. I could split it with Beoreg—his reward for sharing the starter—and his restaurant could have very nice tables, indeed.

I thought about it all the way through Madera, Patterson, Tracy, and Livermore, and when Jaina Mitra pulled her Tesla onto the airfield in Alameda, I had my answer.

"I'm sorry. I can't."

Her face crumpled. "Were we not clear? You have something very, very important."

"I just don't feel like it's *mine* to give. In fact, it's the other way around. You don't understand, because you haven't worked with it. And I heard a story about it—a warning." I paused. "I'm going to get rid of it."

"Please, please, *please* don't do that."

I cracked the passenger-side door. "I'm sure you'll find another way to make your stuff work. A better way."

"Let's keep talking about this!" Jaina Mitra called as I stepped out of the car. She was reaching over, her seat belt cutting into her shoulder, her expression pleading. "Keep that starter. Keep it alive!"

THE ISLAND OF THE MAZG

THAT NIGHT, I SLEPT ON MY FUTON on Cabrillo Street, satisfied with my decision. There were paths ahead that didn't require the Clement Street starter. I still had the Vitruvian, and I had become possibly the world's leading expert on the use of robot automation in kitchen processes.

In the morning, I was startled awake by a bad dream that melted away as soon as I tried to remember it. It was dark outside. I decided I would go to the Marrow Fair and make my peace with the starter. It felt like it should be a private affair.

I rode my bike to the pier and waited for Carl to arrive. The atmosphere was close and clammy, heavy clouds hanging low. Some days, working in the Marrow Fair, I missed the sky, but this would not be one of them. It would be cooler down in the depot.

The *Omebushi* approached the pier, chugging merrily. Aboard, Carl's mood matched mine.

"Haven't seen you in a while," he said, his voice still sticky with sleep. "People said you were spending the night." He poured us both some coffee and launched his boat again.

We cleared the Bay Bridge and rounded Yerba Buena Island on the way to Alameda. Then, we both saw it at the same time.

Ahead, the silhouette of the island had changed. A hazy bulge loomed in the center of the airfield. There was a new structure there—vast, round, and somehow built overnight.

Was this part of Mr. Marrow's grand opening?

The *Omebushi* brought us closer.

Though it was as large as one of the hangars, it wasn't a proper structure, but rather an organic form with a swollen, gaseous look. It might have been a rising hot-air balloon or a crashed dirigible.

Or, as I considered it, an enormous panettone.

Carl muttered a curse. Keeping one hand on the wheel, he dug in the compartment beneath his seat, produced a pair of binoculars, and tossed them into my lap.

Through the binoculars, I could make out the texture of the structure, and a sick feeling bloomed in my gut.

The forgotten lemon I'd discovered in my explorations of the depot's dark corridors—I had picked it up, only to discover that the bottom was fuzzed over with fungus, velvety to the touch. Out of sick curiosity, I'd held my breath and peeled the lemon's skin away to discover that the fungus had padded its interior with airy filaments.

Through the binoculars, I saw that, but huge.

The billowing surface looked velvety like the underside of the lemon, and in the softness there was a pattern of ridges and depressions, and in that pattern, there was the unmistakable swirl of faces.

I put the binoculars down.

I knew those faces.

The *Omebushi* bumped roughly against the tiny pier. "Better get in there and see what's happening," Carl said.

I waved my bone-key token in front of the bay-side door. It called me skinny and unlocked, but when it opened, there was no depot.

Instead, I stared at a wall of the same material that bloomed on the airfield. Pale, creamy, billowing, and patterned with familiar faces. They were variously ecstatic and anguished and accusing and calm.

Up close, the smell was overpowering. Banana and gunpowder.

For a moment I was hypnotized. Then, tentatively, I extended a finger and poked at one of the faces. The substance yielded like foam.

It had the consistency of Lembas.

It *was* Lembas.

Carl was at my side, holding an oar. "Careful there," he said. He prodded the ballooning substance with the butt of the oar and it fell away; behind the Lembas was more Lembas. The depot was full of it.

AGRIPPA'S GOATS WERE CLUSTERED at the edge of the airfield, clearly perturbed by the apocalyptic puff pastry that had invaded their domain. Their keeper stood among them; he looked more placid.

"Agrippa!" I called. "How did this happen?"

"Don't ask me," he said. "The goats woke me up. They were freaking out."

"Have you called anyone?"

"Nope."

I wanted to sputter in protest. I remembered who I was dealing with.

I ran to the control tower, descended the spiral staircase, and waved my bone key. The door opened—*STILL—TOO—SKINNY*—revealing the concourse.

Just inside, my workstation was safe, unaffected. The Vitruvian wobbled apprehensively. The Clement Street starter was quiet in its tub. But farther down the concourse, where Jaina Mitra's lab had been, the Lembas had formed a massive trunk that reached up to grip the ceiling. There, it splayed out in a dramatic many-fingered star, and one of its fingers had found the skylight above the lemon grove and pushed its way through to form the base of the bulbous structure rising on the airfield. Below it, the lemon grove had been consumed entirely. A few dark leaves were suspended in the Lembas like feathers on the nose of a cartoon cat.

The great bloom of Lembas blocked the skylight, so the only illumination came from the grow rooms, which cast their pink glow across a rippling scene that also had a soundtrack: Chaiman's album was playing, and not the spare overture but the later tracks, the ones in which he had accelerated the songs of the Mazg and overlaid them with rising sirens, bursts of noise, and a driving *oonce-oonce-oonce*.

It was a fungal party hellscape.

The Lembas was not finished. Around the absorbed lemon grove, it was growing in hungry surges. Was it obeying the *oonce*s? I watched it bulge sickly in time to the music.

Then a figure darted into view. It was Horace: wielding a wide book, charging forward, poking at the Lembas, slashing it, gaining ground.

Just beyond the grove was his library.

Horace was holding the Lembas at bay.

His shouts echoed. *"Back!"* he hollered. *"Back!"*

I kicked at the brakes on the Vitruvian's wheeled base, spun it around, and pushed forward. We coasted together down the yellow-tape road, the arm's momentum almost overbalancing it as we caromed into workstations and refrigerators before reaching the place where Horace was making his stand. He had his heels set, swiping with the book as the Lembas encircled him, *oonce* by *oonce.*

I locked the Vitruvian's brakes and grabbed at Horace's shirt. "Let the arm do it!" Then, all my scorn for the programmers on Interface drained away as I shouted, "Arm, *change task! Say hello!"* and the Vitruvian began to swing in a wide, slow arc. Where Horace's book had been making scratches, the arm made great gouges. It was tireless. The Lembas could not pass.

I heard a howl and turned to see Stephen Agrippa emerge from the depot's vehicle ramp. He was running, Hercules the alpaca beside him, and all the goats a pace behind. Agrippa urged them forward with feral hoots and yips. Hercules spat.

The Lembas was vast but brittle; where its growth had slowed, it left an airy matrix, like the crumb of one of my loaves but scaled up massively. So, when we struck it—the Vitruvian with its great fist, Hercules with his hooves, Agrippa and I taking swipes with fingers curled into claws—it broke away in ragged chunks that tumbled and bounced to be consumed by the ravenous and, frankly, terrifying goats.

The goats feasted. The Lembas shrank. I reached out, gently now, and brought a sliver of the substance to my tongue. It didn't dissolve into slime or stick to my teeth. This Lembas was a light, crispy bread with a deep well of flavor.

It was . . . really good.

Horace was still swinging with his book, enraged, protecting his archive. I unlocked the Vitruvian's brakes and pushed it slowly forward on its base. Its great swipes sent chunks of Lembas the size of beer kegs arcing slowly through the air.

At last, it was too much. The Lembas could not hold. A thin crack crept up the trunk, then spiderwebbed out, and it all began to fracture, glacierlike, huge slabs coming unstuck. The giant top, deprived of its foundation, came tumbling down—but gently. I tucked my chin into my chest, covered my head with my hands, and held my breath. The collapse was nearly soundless; just the whisper of a Rice Krispies Treat moving against itself.

I peeked. I was covered in the stuff. Everything was covered in the stuff. The smell of bananas was overpowering.

LATER THAT MORNING, the people of the Marrow Fair surveyed the damage in a deep, padded silence. Sometime during the scuffle, Chaiman's album had reached the end of its *oonc*ing and the playlist, mercifully, had not been set to repeat.

The Lembas had filled much of the depot, and Agrippa

was going corridor by corridor with his insatiable goats. Hercules, however, had reached his limit. The alpaca was sitting in the ruin of the lemon grove, apparently asleep.

Horace had successfully defended his archive, and the cricket farm had resisted the Lembas without assistance; there, the wave front stopped abruptly, ragged-edged, gnawed to a standstill by thousands of tiny mouths. The crickets chirped contentedly.

I looked around the depot and for a moment I saw it with Agrippa's eyes. These were the ruins of a glittering, overnight civilization. There were aeons packed into those hours.

More people were milling around the depot now and the spell was breaking. I heard cries of alarm and dismay, and then, increasingly, laughter. Vendors dug out their workstations, checked to see what had been wrecked and what was intact. Our bodies were all coated gray-green with a dusting of Lembas. We might have been made of Lembas ourselves.

Lily Belasco arrived, her lips curling in disbelief that such a disaster could have unfolded on the day before the market's public launch. She conscripted Orli and me to help Naz excavate the coffee bar and return the espresso machine to operational status.

"Quick," she urged. "Quick quick quick."

WE ALL WORKED TOGETHER, hauling the Lembas away in slabs, piling it up like firewood. Finally, we reached the epicenter, and there we found Jaina Mitra, who had scratched out a little cave for herself. I'd expected panic. Instead, she was exultant.

The bioreactor told the tale. The metal twisted apart in a wicked pucker. It had been breached from the inside.

Through the broken skylight, I heard sirens on the airfield.

"You used the starter," I said. "You just took it."

Jaina Mitra nodded, unrepentant. Her eyes flashed white and wild beneath a mask of Lembas dust.

THE FIRE DEPARTMENT blocked off the airfield and set up a perimeter around the control tower, clearing us out of the depot, but there was a languor to their efforts. The bloom was quiescent. In its great leap into the world above, the hybrid Lembas and Clement Street starter seemed to have burned itself out.

The firefighters stood around, not sure what to do. A helicopter hung low overhead. I waved.

"You can eat it," I heard one firefighter say to another.

"*Eat* it?" the other said.

"Yep. Not that I'm gonna. But you can."

All the vendors of the Marrow Fair stood in a loose ring around the control tower, chatting and checking phones.

I saw Jaina Mitra coming around the side of the brewery, leading a scrum of people in lab coats. I recognized one of the figures, tall and scary-skinny: it was Dr. Klamath from Slurry Systems of Fresno, California.

"You're in charge of the market?" he said to Belasco.

"That's right," she said. She was on her fifth espresso and seemed finally to have found her equilibrium.

"I need to assert our intellectual property rights in this matter. We have a claim under the Budapest Treaty . . ."

My Klamath-as-Marrow theory was dashed.

"You'll have to work that out with Mr. Marrow," Belasco said. "I'll pass along your . . . assertion?"

"Please. We have work to do here."

"Work to do!" I rounded on Jaina Mitra. "Did you do this on *purpose*?" I waved at the city-scale panettone.

"Of course not," she said flatly. Her face was still dusted gray-green. "I was terrified. But . . ." She had that Jaina Mitra look in her eye. The gleam. "Consider the *physics* of it. The efficiency . . . I estimated the mass and, even accounting for gas inflation, it's at nearly the thermodynamic optimum. Don't you see? Almost *perfect* conversion."

"Cool, but did you see your bioreactor? It *exploded*."

Dr. Klamath waved his hand dismissively in the direction of the bloom. "We'll build a stronger one. We have to tame it, yes . . . but—that's the breakthrough. We have something to tame! Dr. Mitra found the key."

Did she.

They both looked at me with eyes hard and bright while the tower of pale Lembas behind them glittered in the rising sun.

"Yes, I did." Jaina Mitra said it with the confidence of recitation. "I cultured it myself from freely occurring bacteria in the environment. That's how sourdough starter works, you know."

BECAUSE THE HYBRID LEMBAS was safe to eat, the bloom was ruled not a biohazard, and therefore not subjected to the

246

various quasi-military quarantine procedures that would otherwise have been triggered. The CDC had nothing to say about snacks the size of houses.

The weekend following the bloom, the bridges and tunnels into Alameda were crowded to a standstill and the ferries were packed full with curious residents bringing their families to inspect up close the phenomenon they'd seen from across the bay.

They parked wherever they could find space, cars spilling onto the airfield, and walked across the cracked asphalt to break off a piece of the Lembas and tentatively put it between their lips. A thick swirl of people circled the bloom, levering off large chunks, which were broken into smaller pieces and handed down to children, who liked it most of all. The whole scene was very *Cloudy with a Chance of Meatballs*. Very *Strega Nona*.

An intrepid falafel truck pulled up and began to fry bits of the bloom into a new kind of fritter.

Agrippa and his goats watched from a distance.

Below, the market had its grand opening. It wasn't the one Mr. Marrow had planned; it was ten times better. Fifty thousand people came to Alameda that day.

People sampled cricket cookies and tube-fish tacos and pink-light kale. Every teenager on the airfield gripped one of the smoothies with . . . *things* swimming inside them. I never did find out what those were.

A week passed. Traffic across the Bay Bridge resumed its normal speed as drivers got their fill of the sight. The bloom sagged on the airfield, depleted but still enormous. Even the assembled nibbling power of the Bay Area had left it largely intact.

Klamath's team erected a field laboratory beside it. They were trying to reverse engineer the bloom, determine what had activated it so they could do so again, this time in Fresno, inside a stronger vat. A bigger one, too.

I saw Jaina Mitra stalking the bloom's perimeter, gazing up at it with a hungry expression.

THE LOIS CLUB (CONCLUDED)

IT'S INCREDIBLE," said Hilltop Lois. She held up a newspaper, the struggling local edition, and rattled it for emphasis. On the front page there was an aerial photo of the bloom, and below it, the headline: CLINGSTONE'S MARKET EXPLODES.

Clingstone's . . . ?

"Can I read that?"

I snatched the paper away without waiting for a reply. The whole story of the Marrow Fair was unfurled. The reporter, after some digging in the Alameda County records office, had worked her way through several shell companies to divine the identity of the market's owner.

"Charlotte Clingstone," I read. "This whole time."

"Amazing, isn't it?" Hilltop Lois said.

As I made my way through the story, my stomach gradually unclenched. I'd been expecting to see my own name, but there was no mention of local baker (and/or irresponsible microbial steward) Lois Clary. The story said the source of the "nontoxic environmental disruption" was a runaway experiment by Lembas Labs, which, it explained, had been recently acquired by Slurry Systems of Fresno, California.

Unfortunately, that put Slurry on the hook, liability-wise; several people had gotten sick gorging themselves on Lembas fritters, and a collision on the Bay Bridge was being blamed on the visual distraction of the bloom.

"Are you okay over there?" Compaq Lois called.

I put the paper down and looked at the Loises. "Can I tell you a story?"

In the kitchen, over glasses of port, I unspooled it. I told them about Clement Street Soup and Sourdough and the food I'd loved so intensely, so briefly.

"They gave me something when they left," I said. "It was a gift."

I told them about the starter's growth, and Agrippa and his goats, and the trip to Fresno with Jaina Mitra.

It took an hour to tell it. The Loises listened, rapt.

At the end, they each had a different opinion.

"Maybe you can get your old job back," Professor Lois said.

"Open a new bakery, is what I say." Hilltop Lois thumped her fist on the countertop. "Down in Cole Valley. It's a great neighborhood!"

"What about stock in that company?" Compaq Lois asked. "What was it called? Sludgy? You could sue for that."

Old Lois pursed her lips. She was either annoyed or amused; I couldn't tell. I prodded her. "Well? What do you think?"

"Oh, it's obvious." She smiled smugly. "You must go visit this young man. Beoreg? Yes. Beoreg."

That I did not expect.

"Somebody get a mirror. Lois the Baker, if you could see your own face when you talk about your messages back and forth, you'd know it, too."

Professor Lois started to speak, but Old Lois held up a hand, exquisitely wrinkled, to silence her.

"She needs to go."

There was a vibration in her voice that told a whole story, of Most Respected Elder Lois and some other soul, and a risky journey, long ago. And . . . a reward? A disappointment?

"Go," she said. "It will be worth it." A reward, then.

Hilltop Lois sighed limply. "Well. There are Lois Clubs all over the world."

Old Lois cackled at that. Then another Lois was laughing, and another, and then it was all of us Loises laughing together in a dark-shingled house on the hill behind the hospital with a view of the park and the ocean beyond.

MR. MARROW

I CONFRONTED CHARLOTTE CLINGSTONE in her garden behind Café Candide as she squatted beside a grid of bushy arugula, picking the widest fronds, leaving the others to grow larger.

"It was less a lie," she said languidly, "and more of a considered omission."

She didn't look like the secret impresario of an underground market, dressed now in sturdy jeans and a pink linen shirt with a banded collar, her hair swept back behind a pink headband.

I should have known Mr. Marrow was the kind of person whose headband matched her top.

"Was it just a game?"

Her expression was firm. "I believe everything I ever said as Mr. Marrow. I believe, also, that this restaurant is a precious place. Can't I believe both? I think I can."

"What about 'tending your garden'?"

Clingstone smiled distantly. "Oh, what *about* that book? I still love it. But I also wonder how it could possibly have resonated so powerfully with a twenty-three-year-old who had seen so little of the world. Now that I've actually suffered, I find it somewhat . . . theoretical."

"But why do it all in secret?" Surely, a market known to be organized by Charlotte Clingstone would be a huge deal. Overnight, the Ferry Building itself would have a rival.

Clingstone's gaze turned inward, and more gently she said, "It never occurs to people that maybe I'd like to be the reckless one. The disrupter! As the years have passed, I have discovered in myself this . . . energy. Is it anger? A touch of spite? I'm not sure." She looked back toward the restaurant. The beans on their strings were rippling on a breeze so gentle I couldn't feel it. "I can't be reckless with the café. We directly support twenty-seven farms and ranches. Almost four hundred people! And there's my staff, of course." She looked at me wickedly. "I wanted a place to break things, and that place is my Marrow Fair."

"So what happens now?"

"Now the market is open. We see what succeeds. Oh, and guess what? Through my investment in Jaina Mitra and her Lembas Labs, I now own three percent of a company called Slurry Systems. Isn't that interesting? They say it might be worth a billion dollars." She stood and brushed off her jeans. "You should join us here at the café."

"You can't be serious."

"Why not? Learn from Mona. She'll teach you how to make that sourdough pizza crust we were talking about. You're beyond the novice's grace now."

She wasn't wrong, but this wasn't the place I wanted to learn.

"And I paid for that robot, don't forget. What were the terms again? I think I own twenty percent of your company. If there is a company."

I walked out through the café's burnished dining room, the acolytes setting tables, their shadows moving in the dark wood. It really was a beautiful place. There was a bowl of plums sitting alone on a table. I plucked one out and ate it on the way to the train.

THE BEGINNING

O N FOOD BLOGS and in social media posts, the eaters of
the Bay Area rendered their first judgments of the
Marrow Fair; these ranged from deep appreciation to utter
bafflement. Some people said Charlotte Clingstone had betrayed everything she ever stood for; others said she was
plotting a commendable course for the future. Everyone agreed
the bookstore at the back of the market was a gem.

Horace, spooked by the near loss of his archive, finally
pieced together a book proposal and sold it to a publisher in
Berkeley. He was to write a wide-ranging literary history of
eating. It was to be finished in two years. His face was pale
when he told me.

Jaina Mitra and Dr. Klamath retreated to Fresno with a
sample of the substance that had bloomed above the Marrow
Fair. They would become acquainted with the Clement Street
starter now, and record their own catalog of phenomena.
They would learn a lot using their sequencers and bioreac-
tors, but would they ever suspect the crucial role that music
played? Maybe I'd send them a clue. Maybe not.

In Berlin, Beoreg had opened his restaurant. He sent me

a picture of the space he'd leased in Kreuzberg. It was no larger than my apartment, but it faced a busy street, and inside, there were three tiny, glorious tables. The process had not been without intra-Mazg drama, but Beo was undeterred.

Out of necessity, I read the very first chapter of *The Soul of Sourdough*, the one I'd skipped, about capturing a wild starter. Following Everett Broom's instructions, I set a dish of flour and water on the windowsill and watched it closely. Within a week, it was bubbling. And that's all it did, ever. This sourdough starter was a party of two, just yeast and lactobacillus, like every other starter in the world except for one.

I returned to the Jay Steve Value Oven in the backyard. In my absence, the Cabrillo Street cats had made it into their lair. I shooed them away and built a fire. Cornelia came outside and watched me learn to bake again for the first time. Mainly, we sat in companionable silence. Then, one morning, after we'd pulled a couple of particularly plump loaves from the Jay Steve, I told her I was leaving.

"A lot of people have lived in that apartment," she said, "but none of them ever fed me before you came along."

I told her I'd leave her some of the starter so she could bake her own bread.

She narrowed her eyes. "What am I getting myself into? Is it high-maintenance? I don't like high-maintenance."

"Not this one," I said. "It's boring."

THERE'S A CRATE HERE at the restaurant in Kreuzberg. It's enormous, and it's addressed to NUMBER ONE EATER. Is it a mistake? Are you inside the crate? I banged on it and called your name, but there was no reply. Then I pried it open (sorry), but there was just another box inside. This one is bright blue, with a lightning bolt.

Lois, what's going on?

BEO! Inside that big blue box there is a refurbished Vitruvian 3 robot arm, partially disassembled, loaded with software I helped create. That robot and I have been through a lot together. I have things to teach it still.

I'm coming to Berlin.

I'm starting a new business, and I need your help. I want to learn how to use knives correctly, and which vegetables are which, and how to make my own spicy soup. (That's not a euphemism.) (It could be a euphemism.) If you can teach me, I can teach the Vitruvian, and then those skills can be shared in a new way, thanks to my former employer. The world is going to change, I think—slowly at first, then faster than anyone expects. It's going to be a weird time, but along the way I think I can get rich. *We* can get rich.

Beo, I'll bring plenty of Fresno chilies.

I also want to learn how to bake sourdough the way you did on Clement Street. Honestly, mine was never as good. But I have one condition, and you might not like it.

Let's not use the starter of the Mazg.

It almost caught me, Beo. And then it caught someone

else. It starts out very sweetly, doesn't it? The songs, the smiles. One night, I saw a dusting of pinprick lights. Luminous powdered sugar. That feels like a long time ago. Maybe, if you're lucky (or if you're you), the starter of the Mazg stays sweet. But if you're not, it sneaks up on you—the ambition, the impatience, the *hunger* . . . I'll tell you the whole story when I get to Berlin. There aren't any pirates in this one, but it does feature a great rocky island, along with some very heroic goats.

This time, I'm bringing *you* a starter: authentic San Francisco sourdough, native citizen of Cabrillo Street. I captured it myself. I will decant it into a plastic container small enough to take through airport security. If challenged, I will claim it's moisturizer.

In Berlin, it will grow.

It will make no faces and sing no songs, but I guarantee you, it will do its part. And, Beo, working there with you, I will set myself, at last, to the task of learning mine.

Printed in the USA
CPSIA information can be obtained
at www.ICGtesting.com
LVHW051034050823
754287LV00005B/995

9 781250 192752